Pamela sat up and r̶ ̶ ̶ ̶ ̶ ̶ ̶ ̶ ̶ ̶ ̶ ̶ ̶ ̶ ̶ ̶ ̶ ̶ ̶ from her face, and that was when she saw it.

Two harsh, angry, unyielding eyes, glowing across the fire from her. The man who stared back at her was not Bradley! Nervously, Pamela scooted back a bit before demanding to know the man's identity.

"Who are you? Where's Bradley?" she asked as forcefully as she could.

The man did nothing for a minute. He just kept staring at her with eyes that would yield nothing more than something that closely resembled hatred. His lean, angular jaw was clenched tightly, so tightly in fact that Pamela could see a noticeable ticking in his cheek.

"Well?" she pressed for an answer.

"I might ask you the same," the deep voice sounded from across the flames.

"I presumed you knew. Didn't you help Bradley rescue me?" Pamela asked innocently.

"I don't know what you're talking about, lady." The man sprung to his feet like a circus cat performing its paces. Pamela shrank away. Her heart was beating wildly. Who was this man?

"I'm talking about this," Pamela finally offered in a weak voice. She waved her arm across the sky. "My rescue."

"I didn't plan to rescue you. I don't know who this Bradley is, and I sure don't know who you are." He came to stand no more than a foot or so away from her before he crouched down. "Who are you?"

Pamela began to tremble....

TRACIE J. PETERSON is a popular inspirational writer and a regular columnist for a Christian newspaper in Topeka, Kansas. Tracie has also written eight successful **Heartsong Presents** titles under the name of Janelle Jamison.

HEARTSONG PRESENTS

Books by Janelle Jamison

Books by Tracie J. Peterson

Don't miss out on any of our super romances. Write to us at the following address for information on our newest releases and club information.

Heartsong Presents Readers' Service
P.O. Box 719
Uhrichsville, OH 44683

The Heart's
Calling

Tracie J. Peterson

Heartsong Presents

Dedicated to my Grandmother Williams,
who shared many stories with me
of her childhood and the good ol' days.
I love you, Grandma!

A note from the Author:
I love to hear from my readers! You may correspond
with me by writing:

Tracie J. Peterson
Author Relations
P.O. Box 719
Uhrichsville, OH 44683

ISBN 1-55748-667-0

THE HEART'S CALLING

one

"Do you have everything you need, my dear?"

Her grandmother's heavy French accent only increased Pamela Charbonneau's misery. "I have nothing at all," she pouted.

Claudia Charbonneau shrugged her shoulders. "Life is what one makes it, *n'est-ce pas?*"

"No, it isn't so," Pamela insisted, tossing her stylish blond curls from side to side. Only an hour earlier, Claudia's own maid had painstakingly pinned and curled Pamela's waist-length hair, and now she threatened to bring it all back down with her childish tantrum. "I'm eighteen years old, and so far my life is only what others force upon me. I am not allowed to make my life my own!"

"*Ma petite fille*, you bring most of the trouble upon yourself."

"But *Grand-mère*," Pamela interrupted, "I'm in love, and my parents don't understand. Bradley Rayburn means the world to me. My parents were cruel and vicious to make me leave him and Kansas City. It's my home, and he's the man I intend to marry."

"Marry him?" Claudia Charbonneau replied, with her first show of disgust. "I cannot see why a young woman such as yourself would want to settle down to marriage and the unpleasantness of childbearing before you have a chance to see the world and all that it has to offer. Perhaps then your Bradley Rayburn would hold less fascination for you."

"Impossible," Pamela protested, bringing herself up to her full five-foot, two-inch height. Claudia was no taller than her granddaughter, but because of her elegance and refinement Pamela felt as though the woman towered over her by a foot.

"I love him!" Pamela cried. "I will always love him, and as soon as I can figure a way to leave this south Missouri hick town, I will!"

Claudia was not impressed by her granddaughter's show of temper. It was all to be expected. Pamela's parents had never spent enough time at home to rear the child when she was young, so she had learned her values and principles from nannies and house staff. When her father and mother finally reappeared, it was just in time to find a local ne'er-do-well dandy keeping company with their daughter—and with the audacious intention of marrying her!

"It would be well if you learned to appreciate this town for its quiet reserve and charm," Claudia was saying, but Pamela had angrily turned away.

"I hate it here, already," Pamela muttered, and whirled on her heel. "Nobody loves me! Nobody but Bradley!" With that Pamela threw herself across the feather mattress of her bed and cried.

Claudia Charbonneau shook her head and left her grand-daughter to have her cry. It was the fourth that day. Sooner or later, Pamela would have to understand that what was done was done, and no amount of tears would change that fact.

At noon, Pamela finally emerged from her bedroom to join her grandmother for lunch. She sat at the opposite end of the elegant table, watching her grandmother instruct her servants in a low voice, her words inaudible to Pamela.

When Claudia finished, she gave Pamela a polite nod and lifted a sterling fork. "Shall we begin?"

Pamela ate in miserable silence. Her grandmother had instructed her only that morning that too much conversation at the dinner table would lead to upsetting the delicate balance of one's stomach. Pamela was full to the rim of her reddened eyes with rules that her grandmother intended her to follow.

She was not to leave the house unescorted.

She was not to drink anything cooler than room temperature.

She was not, under any circumstance, to appear outside of the house before ten o'clock in the morning, and she was never to speak to anyone before Claudia's introduction.

Rules, rules, rules! Pamela thought she'd burst from frustration. At least in Kansas City there hadn't been a list of rules to follow. Her parents traveled abroad so often that Pamela had had a free rein. The servants adored her, and she in turn bestowed on them the love she would have given her parents, had they been around to receive it.

Now she was here—and she wasn't even sure where *here* really was. She'd been forced to take the train south from Kansas City and then travel by stage to this small Missouri community where her grandmother had spent the last few years. All this traveling was in order to separate her from Bradley.

Oh, Bradley! Pamela sighed, remembering his boyish smile and curly blond hair. Friends had teased her, saying she would have nothing but blond-headed babies and that, because she and Bradley were such a handsome couple, their children would no doubt be beautiful.

Lifting a forkful of curried chicken to her mouth, Pamela ate while barely tasting the food. Although the scene her parents had caused on the night of her engagement party was almost more than Pamela could bear to remember, she could not help thinking about it.

They were supposed to be in New York for at least another week, and Pamela had planned an elaborate party at which to announce her engagement. She reasoned that her parents couldn't possibly tell her "no" after all Kansas City's social elite turned out to wish her and Bradley well. But something had happened to bring them home early. Perhaps they'd caught wind of the party, or maybe someone had deliberately sent for them. Either way, Pamela would never forgive her father for the way he had barged into the formal dining room, where forty people were celebrating her engagement, and announced that there would be no wedding. If that weren't bad enough, he had ordered Bradley thrown out of the house and Pamela to her room.

"He treated me like a child," Pamela muttered.

"Did you say something?" Claudia asked, with a look of annoyance.

Pamela stiffened. "No," she lied. "I was just thinking aloud."

So her life went on that January of 1883. Pamela was a prisoner in her grandmother's home while Bradley was somewhere in Kansas City, no doubt nursing a broken heart.

&

Alexandra Dawson—Zandy to her friends and family— finished buttoning her burgundy wool coat before seeking out her husband.

"I'm ready to go," she said, entering the manly confines of Riley Dawson's office.

"Not without a kiss," he said and patted his lap. Zandy smiled and quickly crossed the room to comply.

"I wouldn't dream of it," she whispered against his ear.

Hugging her close, Riley couldn't help but feel as though he were the most blessed man in the world. Not that long ago, he had confronted Zandy with the experience of seeing him for the first time in over a year. To make matters worse, the encounter took place after she had thought him dead and buried.

"What are you thinking?" she asked, pulling back just far enough to meet his brown-black eyes.

"Just how very good God has been to me," Riley answered.

Zandy appreciated his words of praise for God, especially remembering how adamantly Riley had rejected Him when they had first met.

"It seems hard to believe that I'm the same man who gambled his way into ownership of a Colorado mining town and tried to force his attentions on one young, beautiful, and very naive girl."

"I was not naive!" Zandy protested. "You didn't get what you wanted, did you?"

Riley laughed. "As a matter of fact, I did. I just didn't get it the way I intended."

Zandy joined his laughter. "No, God had other plans for you, Riley Dawson, and making me your mistress wasn't one of them. You may own enough silver mines to pave the streets of Denver, but when you deal with me, you deal with my God."

"Our God," Riley said, in a contented way that warmed

Zandy's heart.

"Yes," she murmured. "Our God."

Riley pulled her face down to meet his and kissed her long and lovingly. Zandy snuggled up against him like a child being cradled.

"I thought you were going into town," Riley mused.

"I am."

"It doesn't appear that way to me," he teased.

"Shows what you know," Zandy countered, with a twinkle in her green eyes. "I'm already halfway down the street."

Riley laughed and put her from his lap. "You'd best get on your way before I decide you shouldn't go out on a cold day like this."

"As if that would stop me," Zandy called over her shoulder. "By the way," she added, as she paused at the door, "do you need anything?"

"Only you," Riley replied, and pushed back the black hair that had fallen over one eye.

"I believe you could use a haircut. Maybe you should come with me," Zandy offered.

Riley shook his head. "No, I've got to see to these accounts. Your father is doing a fine job of managing the city of Dawson for us, but he always feels better when I give him my report on the matter. You run along, and when you get back I'll play you a game of chess." Zandy nodded and happily took herself off to do her shopping.

❧

Zandy entered Mrs. Mallory's dress shop at exactly eleven o'clock. She had promised to come for a dress fitting, and Mrs. Mallory hated it when anyone was as much as a minute late.

"Good morning, Mrs. Mallory," Zandy said, pulling off her black leather gloves.

"Good morning, Mrs. Dawson. I have your dress nearly finished," the heavyset woman said, coming to help Zandy off with her coat. "You know where to change your clothes. I'll bring the dress to you shortly."

Zandy nodded and took herself into the small adjoining fitting room. She quickly stepped out of her blouse and skirt and accepted the new creation of cream-colored velvet.

"I'll do up the buttons for you," Mrs. Mallory said, taking Zandy in hand as though she were a small child. "You have such a fine figure to work with. Pity I can't take more after you and less after my husband."

Zandy giggled slightly at the reference to Mrs. Mallory's portly husband. "You have a grace that poor Mister Mallory could never hope to achieve."

Mrs. Mallory smiled and stepped back to survey her work. "Yes, this looks perfect."

Zandy couldn't see the mirror from where she stood, but she liked the feel of the gown and knew that Mrs. Mallory wasn't one to offer idle praise.

The older woman worked diligently at the task of tacking black jets to the bodice and finished by taking a final tuck in the waist.

"I'll have it ready on Saturday," Mrs. Mallory said abruptly. She unbuttoned the gown and moved away. "You may change now."

Zandy was used to these curt dismissals from her dressmaker. Mrs. Mallory was one of the few people in town who didn't love to spend hours chatting about nothing in particular.

Zandy quickly replaced the elegant gown with her more durable blue wool skirt and white blouse. She had just reentered the front room when the bell on the door sounded and two women entered.

"Mrs. Charbonneau," Zandy said, extending her hand to the older woman. "I was going to stop by today and thank you for the invitation to dinner and, of course, to accept."

"Madame Dawson," Claudia remarked with a smile, "it is always a pleasure to speak with you. Might I introduce my granddaughter? This is Pamela Charbonneau, formerly of Kansas City."

Zandy's eyes left the older woman and traveled to the obviously miserable younger one. "Miss Charbonneau, it's wonderful to make your acquaintance."

"Mrs. Dawson," Pamela said with a questioning interest. This woman couldn't be much older than she was.

"Please, call me Zandy. May I call you Pamela?"

"Please do," Pamela replied. She immediately liked Zandy and saw the possibility of a friendship.

"I must be on my way," Zandy announced, pulling on her coat, "but, I wonder, would you like to stop by for tea this afternoon?"

"Oh my," Claudia said, holding a lace-edged handkerchief to her throat. "I know I won't have the energy for such an outing, but perhaps Pamela would enjoy it. I would so like for her to spend time getting to know you."

Pamela perked up at the thought of an afternoon spent anywhere but in the austere Charbonneau mansion. "I'd love to. Thank you, Mrs. Dawson. I mean, Zandy."

"Good. I'll expect you at three," Zandy bade the women goodbye and went to finish her rounds in town.

At three o'clock, Pamela arrived in a hansom carriage of lacquered black and gold. She felt as though a yoke had been lifted from her neck as she approached the cobblestone walkway that led to the Dawson mansion. It was an impressive two-storied house of natural stone, with a black wrought-iron fence surrounding the yard.

Bradley and I could have had something like this, she thought. *What am I saying? We'll still have something like this. I'll find a way to get back to Kansas City. Maybe Mrs. Dawson can even help me.* The thoughts ran in whirlwinds in Pamela's mind as she reached out and sounded the brass door knocker.

Expecting an old butler, Pamela opened her mouth in surprise at the sight of Riley Dawson. He made a dashing figure in his navy blue afternoon suit. She didn't know who this dark-headed man was, but he was certainly handsome.

"Miss Charbonneau, I presume," Riley said extending his hand. "I'm Riley Dawson, Zandy's husband."

Pamela eased her gloved hand into Riley's. "I'm pleased to meet you, Mister Dawson."

Riley smiled, revealing perfect white teeth. The glint in his eyes made it clear he was a man who enjoyed life. "Call me Riley, and come inside, please. It's much too cold to stand gabbing on the steps."

Pamela allowed Riley to usher her to the sitting room, where Zandy was already fussing over the tea. "Pamela!" she exclaimed and quickly crossed the room. "I'm so glad you could come."

"Me too. I was beginning to fret that there would be no one my own age in this town," Pamela confessed.

Zandy laughed. "I know full well what you mean. This seems to be a community of stately, refined characters, who have nothing better to do than garden and take naps. But it is a wonderful town. So peaceful and simple. Riley and I have grown to love it dearly."

Pamela tried to catch Zandy's enthusiasm but could only nod.

"Riley, take Pamela's coat and we'll have tea," Zandy instructed.

Pamela stayed for over an hour and thoroughly enjoyed herself. She found that once the formalities dropped away, Riley and Zandy were entertaining companions and more than accepting of her. She even relayed a bit of her plight and why she'd come to stay with her grandmother.

"I'm afraid my parents don't understand that the heart's calling can't be controlled. And just because my parents don't approve," Pamela said as Riley helped her into her coat, "doesn't change those feelings."

"Maybe you will change their minds," Zandy replied. "Until then, you're welcome to come and visit as often as you like."

"Thank you, Zandy, Riley. I will call again."

✤

And she did. Pamela found one excuse or another to make her way to the Dawson house nearly every day. Pamela and Zandy laughed about girlhood experiences until they felt that they'd known one another all their lives. Pamela was only a few years junior to Zandy, who found that the company of a young woman was something that had been missing in her life lately.

"I really like her, Riley," Zandy said one evening as they prepared to retire. She sat brushing her long brown hair, while Riley watched from the bed. It was a habit he'd fallen into, and he now realized it was as much a part of his bedtime routine as putting on his night clothes.

"I worry that you're spending too much time together," Riley finally said.

His words surprised Zandy so much she stopped in mid-stroke. "Why do you say that?"

"Well, she's here almost every day. And I can't help but think that you do too much to encourage her when it comes to this Bradley guy."

"Riley Dawson!" Zandy exclaimed. "You, more than anyone, should understand about falling in love with someone. Especially, I might add, someone that you can't have." The coy smile on her lips told him she wasn't really annoyed.

The look on Riley's face told her that he, too, remembered a time when he had actively pursued her, in spite of Zandy's own protests. *But that was different*, he reasoned silently.

Riley patted the mattress beside him, and Zandy put the brush away and joined her husband. "I just don't want you getting involved in something that's better left to others. This is a problem between Pamela and her folks. You have to remember, you aren't her school chum. You're a respectable married woman, and you shouldn't offer too much advice to a young, innocent woman like Pamela."

Zandy stared in surprise at Riley's mild reproof. "I may be married, but I'm not so old that I can't appreciate the company of a young, single woman. I enjoy hearing about her life. She's known so much and lived in a way that I can't begin to understand. Do you know that every stitch of clothing she owns was made in either Paris or New York?"

Riley pulled Zandy into his arms and nuzzled his lips against her ear. "Would you like me to take you to Paris so you can have your gowns made there, too?"

Zandy melted against him with a sigh. "No, Mrs. Mallory would never speak to me again. I just find Pamela stimulating, and I believe her parents are wrong to keep her from the man she loves."

"Be careful, Zandy," Riley warned softly. "You can cause grievous damage by interfering." He gently turned her face to his. "I know how tenderhearted you are, and I don't want to see you hurt. Be her friend, but don't try to be her heart in this matter. Pamela must choose for herself how she'll deal with this situation."

"You're right, of course," Zandy sighed.

"I always am," Riley teased, and he reached over to turn down the lamp.

two

"Wait until you hear this one!" Pamela exclaimed.

Pamela's enthusiasm for her most recent epistle from home caused Riley to roll his eyes. Zandy caught sight of the exasperation in her husband's expression but said nothing.

Pamela made a regular habit of sharing her mail from Kansas City with Zandy, and because of the frequency of her visits Riley had found himself trapped into being a part of their afternoon gatherings on more than one occasion. Today was no exception.

Zandy took the cup of tea that Riley offered her and delicately balanced it against her emerald green day dress. The color matched her eyes and Riley often told her that he fancied the shade on her. Today, however, it seemed to do little to appease his frustration with Pamela.

"Glady, she was my maid," Pamela said, glancing up from the letter, "says that Mama and Papa were home for a short time last week. They were positively in a rage because they had been forced to endure the company of Horace Tabor, the notorious Silver King of Leadville, Colorado."

"I know of Tabor," Riley commented. "He's managed to make a fortune in silver. Nothing overly notorious about that."

"Oh, but it isn't his wealth that put Mama into the vapors," Pamela laughed. "It seems that Mister Tabor has

17

not only a wife and child, but a mistress." Pamela continued reading and didn't notice the way Riley blanched at the word "mistress."

"Mama told Glady that Tabor seems most open about his affair and doesn't care one thing for propriety. She was absolutely mortified. Seems she told Glady that his mistress is quite willing to be the other woman. Mama couldn't abide even the sight of Mister Tabor and told Papa that all such men should be lined up and shot."

At this Riley nearly spewed his tea across the room and brought even more attention to himself by breaking into a fit of coughing. Zandy glanced up, concern flooding her face for only a moment. Catching Riley's eye, amusement seemed to overtake her, and she grinned broadly.

"Yes, I quite agree with your mother," Zandy mused, while Pamela found their byplay most curious. "Such lack of character is appalling. Do go on, Pamela."

"Well, there isn't much more. They say absolutely nothing about Bradley. Oh, Zandy," she sighed and let the letter drop to her lap, "do you suppose I shall ever hear from him?"

"I doubt that your grandmother would allow it," Zandy replied honestly. "Even if you managed to get a letter to him, you know she'd never allow you to receive a reply."

"Yes, I know you're right."

"Why don't we just put it behind us and enjoy our tea," Zandy suggested.

Pamela refolded the letter and put it inside her purse. Just then, a knock at the front door drew Riley's attention, and he found a perfect reason to excuse himself.

"Riley certainly isn't himself today," Pamela said, absent mindedly playing with her teaspoon.

"Oh, he's just a bit on edge," Zandy remarked with a glance at the door. "I'm afraid we ought to cut this session short today. I've been neglecting him sorely."

"Oh," Pamela replied. She felt a bit put out to know that she'd have to return to her grandmother's house so soon.

Seeing her friend's disappointment, Zandy pushed on to offer some consolation. "Why don't we get together tomorrow and go shopping? I have several things I need to pick up."

"Why don't you have the servants see to it?" Pamela asked in a rather haughty tone.

Zandy frowned, realizing that the girl was every bit as spoiled as Riley had mentioned that morning at breakfast. "I enjoy doing for myself," Zandy answered gently. "Sometimes, it is more gratifying to work with your own hands and accomplish something important than to have others do it for you. Now, shopping isn't all that important, but I enjoy it. If you don't wish to go along, that's entirely up to you."

Pamela put her teacup aside and shook her head vehemently. "No, no. I would very much like to accompany you. I certainly didn't mean to offend you."

"You didn't," Zandy smiled. Hearing Riley in the hallway, she quickly stood. "Shall we continue our talk tomorrow, then?"

Pamela reluctantly nodded. "I'll see myself out. You attend to that neglected husband." Her attempt at a smile was forced, but Zandy pretended not to notice.

Riley passed Pamela on the way out and although he raised his brows in a questioning glance, he didn't attempt to stop her departure. The fact was, he had been trying desperately to figure some way to hasten it.

At the sound of the front door closing, Riley crossed the sitting room to where Zandy waited and pulled back the edge of the lacy priscilla curtain. "How did you manage this?" he asked, watching to make certain Pamela was really on her way down the street.

"I told her I'd been neglecting you," Zandy smiled.

"And so you have," Riley answered, letting the curtain fall back into place. "I was beginning to despair of ever having a moment alone with you again."

"Now, Riley," Zandy said, coming to place her hand upon his arm, "there isn't any need for you to sulk. I got rid of her, didn't I? By the way, who was at the door?"

"Just the delivery boy from Nelson's shoe shop," Riley replied. "I ordered a pair of boots some weeks back, and they arrived today."

"Are you expecting any more deliveries?" Zandy asked with a flirtatious smile.

Riley immediately caught her mood. "Why no, Mrs. Dawson. I believe that's the last of them."

"Good. Then we have the house to ourselves," Zandy said sweetly. "And the day."

"And just what do you have planned, my dear Alexandra?" he asked with a chuckle.

Zandy laughed. "No plans. Not yet, anyway. But, I'm sure we'll think of something."

⮿

Pamela Charbonneau was a young woman used to getting her way and, while she knew it was in poor taste to spend so much time at the Dawson house, she couldn't bring herself to do otherwise. She'd even taken to lying to her grandmother in order to avoid a scolding from her on the matter of social politeness.

Throwing herself across her bed and rolling over, Pamela stared up at the floral canopy and sighed.

"Where are you Bradley? You promised you'd come for me. You promised you'd never leave me. Where are you?" The words bounced off the nearly empty walls, leaving Pamela more depressed than ever.

&

The next day, Zandy arrived in a stylish one-horse gig. She hadn't even the time to alight before Pamela appeared on the doorstep, fully prepared for their outing.

Zandy smiled and waved, still preparing to dismount and greet Claudia Charbonneau before their trip, but Pamela would have no part of it.

"*Grand-mère* isn't feeling well," she lied to Zandy. "I'll give her your best when we return."

"Perhaps we shouldn't leave her alone," Zandy said, reseating herself and pulling wool blankets around her legs.

"No, she'll be fine," Pamela said with a smile. "She's just feeling her age today." It wasn't really a lie, Pamela told herself. After all, her grandmother had complained just that morning of how the cold made her bones ache.

"Well, if you're sure."

"Of course, I'm sure," Pamela replied and dismissed any further thought of the matter.

They spent the day shopping and discussing unimportant matters. Zandy had promised Riley that she'd find a way to talk to Pamela about her frequent visits. She fretted over the idea, however, given Pamela's state of depression over the loss of her Bradley. What if losing her constant contact with Zandy was too much for the girl?

When they finally decided to wrap up the day by having lunch, Zandy found herself praying that God would help her to know what to say.

"I'm positively famished," Zandy said and took the menu offered her by the waiter.

Pamela said nothing, but glanced at the list of offered foods and finally settled on petite chicken salad sandwiches. Zandy thought the choice an excellent one and nodded in agreement before the waiter left to bring their tea.

"Might I ask a forward question?" Pamela said suddenly, catching Zandy off guard.

"I suppose so."

"I was curious as to why Riley acted so disturbed yesterday when I mentioned Mister Tabor. Does he know him well?"

Zandy smiled and set her gloves aside. "No, he doesn't know him well at all. Riley Dawson is a most fascinating man," Zandy went on. "When I first met him in Colorado, he was a man of power and control, just coming into his own. He had holdings that gave him control over a small mining town and he pushed that advantage until he'd built a solid investment."

"I'm afraid that still doesn't explain his reaction," Pamela interrupted.

"Riley wasn't at all interested in doing things properly or in a morally right way. He was a godless man with little concern for the human lives he so completely controlled. If ever there was a notorious man, Riley Dawson was certainly one."

Pamela's eyes widened in surprise, but she held her tongue, hoping that Zandy would continue.

"He forced his will upon the people of Temperance, Colorado, and did so in such a remarkably smooth manner that the people didn't even know they'd been had. In fact, they renamed the town Dawson, after Riley, and then elected him mayor. The one thing that eluded Riley—and the one thing he wouldn't give up pursuit of—was me."

Pamela smiled, thinking the whole thing most romantic. Zandy paused long enough to wait until their tea was served before continuing.

"Riley wanted a mistress, Pamela. Not a wife." The shocked expression on Pamela's face told Zandy she'd made her point. "Riley cared nothing about my feelings on the matter, but he did pride himself on the fact that women came willingly to him. I did not, and that moved him to take ugly measures that caused great harm to those I loved."

"How could you possibly have married him?" Pamela asked in disgust.

"I asked myself that about a thousand times. God seemed to have a purpose in mind, and I was very much up against the wall when I finally gave in. I knew it wasn't right to marry an unbeliever, but I reasoned that maybe it was God's way of getting Riley saved."

"Saved?" Pamela questioned ignorantly.

"You know," Zandy said with a smile, "saved from hell. I thought God was using me to guide Riley to salvation in Jesus Christ. Truth be told, He was. Riley became most miserable that he'd forced me into a loveless marriage and, even though we were man and wife, he couldn't bring himself even to sleep in the same house with me."

Pamela's mouth formed a silent "*O*."

"Now, I realize this is a most delicate topic," Zandy continued, "but I use it to share with you just how gracious God was to us and how He worked in Riley's life."

The waiter appeared with their sandwiches, and again Zandy allowed the conversation to halt until they were alone. Pamela picked at her food, eager for Zandy to continue her story.

"One day, Riley took me to visit one of his new silver mines," Zandy remembered, and in her eyes Pamela saw a look of pain. "There was a cave-in and Riley was injured seriously. We were buried inside the mine for days, until the people of Dawson dug us out. My folks had me taken to their house, while Riley was taken to the doctor's. I was sick with exhaustion and weakness for a time, and when I came to they told me Riley had died."

"Died?" Pamela exclaimed, dropping the sandwich. She realized her voice was louder than she'd intended. "Died?" she questioned in a softer tone, looking around to make sure no one was watching them.

"Yes," Zandy answered. "At least, that was what they told me. In truth, Riley knew he had to come to an understanding with God. He'd accepted Christ while thinking that he was going to die in the mine. Then, as he healed, he was afraid to believe in the reality of it because he feared it was nothing more than a deathbed confession. He couldn't face me again until he knew for certain that his faith was real, so he allowed the townspeople to believe he had died."

"What did he do then?" Pamela asked.

"He went about righting the wrongs of his past life. I didn't see him for over a year, and in all that time I never dreamed he was alive. I tried to make amends for Riley's behavior myself. I gave back to the people of Dawson their money and deeds. Whatever Riley had stolen from them, I sought to return. Then I came here to Missouri, opened the boardinghouse that sits on the west end of town, and tried to start life anew.

"It was a truly bleak time for me for, while I knew God

had control of everything, including my widowhood, I was lonely and sad that I'd never really known who Riley Dawson was. One day, he reappeared and begged my forgiveness and told me just what I've told you. It was like being given a second chance at life. That was just last fall, Pamela, and Riley has become the most important person in my life. In fact," Zandy took a sip of tea to settle her nerves, "I had scarcely even spent time with another person before you came to town. It's one of the reasons we haven't any servants, except for the cook. We wanted the privacy." Her teacup rattled slightly as she placed it on the saucer.

Pamela ate on without realizing what Zandy was trying to say. She found it amazing that a man as horrible as Zandy had described could be the same man who welcomed her into his parlor for casual visits.

Zandy knew that Pamela was still blind to her purpose. "Pamela, I've enjoyed our friendship and hope to continue to do so, but I mustn't put a wedge into the tender union that has been formed between Riley and me. We are still, in many ways, newlyweds, and I need time with him to come to know him better. Do you understand?"

"I'm not sure," Pamela replied, dabbing her lips with her napkin. "What has this to do with me?"

"I'm afraid there is no easy way to say this, but to just come out and say it," Zandy sighed. "It would be best if you were to limit your visits to once a week. I don't want to jeopardize our friendship, but I can't put Riley off, either. I'm blessed in the fact that I have his company on a daily basis, and I know that before long he will no doubt find some new project to absorb his time."

Zandy paused, trying to figure out what Pamela was

thinking. "But, until then, I need to spend most of my time with him. It's what we both want and need."

"I see," Pamela said, feeling a warm blush creep to her cheeks. She hadn't expected this turn of events. How could she convince Zandy and Riley to help her get back to Kansas City now?

"Please don't be offended," Zandy said, reaching out to squeeze Pamela's hand. "I want very much for us to continue on as friends. In fact, I was hoping that perhaps you would also attend church with us in the near future. We have some wonderful services and so much fun at the socials. The meetings are enlightening, and the pastor is a truly remarkable man."

Pamela felt a deep aching in her heart. It wasn't the first time that Zandy had spoken of God with such joy. "Does going to church really make life better?"

Zandy recognized the longing in her question. "It isn't so much attending church, although I can't imagine being without Christians to fellowship with. It's the love of God in your life. It's being forgiven for all the wrongs you've ever committed. It's knowing that you have a friend, a Savior, in Jesus Christ and that you never have to be alone again."

"Truly?" Pamela's childish snobbery fell away for the first time.

"Truly."

"And how can you be sure it will work for everyone that way?" Pamela asked sincerely.

"Look at Riley. God completely changed him. Riley was as hopeless as a human being could be, but God found him worth saving and didn't let go until He had him securely in the fold."

"I just don't know," Pamela said, shaking her head. "I've never heard tell of such things. I know from the talks we've had in the past that God is important to you and Riley. I remember your telling me about the peace God gives you but, Zandy, can He honestly take away the pain?" There were tears in Pamela's eyes as the walls of her isolation caved in. "I hurt so much."

Zandy smiled sympathetically. "I know. And, yes, He can take that pain away. Perhaps more important, though, is He will stay with you through the bad times. And, if you let Him, He'll fill the void in your heart with peace and love that is born of Him."

Pamela sobbed softly into her napkin and nodded her head across the table. "Then, do show me how I can be like you."

"Not like me," Zandy replied softly, "like Him."

three

The first of March roared in like a lion, and icy snows pelted everything in sight. The next day, the sun came out and melted the frozen wonderland until all that remained was a brown, muddy mess and the fervent hope of spring.

It was during this time that a letter was delivered to Zandy and Riley that caused them much concern. Burley Stewart, Zandy's father and current mayor of Dawson, Colorado, wrote to tell his daughter and son-in-law that things were not as they should be. He cited complications with the miners and an onslaught of lawlessness that put him in fear of even letting the children walk to school.

Riley read over the letter, handing each page to Zandy after he'd finished. She, in turn, devoured the news with fear and apprehension for her family.

"This is awful, Riley," she said, glancing up from the last sheet of paper. "Father says that a gang of outlaws continues to elude capture, and that they've even harmed some miners in order to steal their silver."

Riley nodded somberly, knowing full well what the letter said.

Zandy quickly finished reading and handed the pages back to her husband. "What are we going to do about this?"

"I don't know." Riley's tone took on the weight of the world. "I've been unhappy for some time about the reports Burley sent. There has been a continuing downward spiral in the quality of our little community. While all mining towns have their share of disorder and lawbreaking, my heart tells me we shouldn't be a part of it any more than we have to."

Zandy waited for Riley to say more but, when he fell into a thoughtful silence, she eagerly picked up the conversation.

"Perhaps God is directing us to get out of the business of silver mining. Mining always attracts a rowdier group of citizens, what with the saloons, gaming houses, and such. Someone is always looking for an easy way to make money. The proof is in the fact that this outlaw gang seems to hold the town hostage at times."

Riley grimaced and stretched his long legs before him. He rubbed his chin thoughtfully while contemplating Zandy's words. "I think we should go to Dawson," he finally said.

Zandy's eye lit up. Not because she wanted to see Dawson, Colorado, but because going would mean seeing her father and stepmother, not to mention her young siblings.

"I think that would be wonderful!" she exclaimed. "How soon could we leave?"

Riley smiled at Zandy's enthusiasm for a family visit, but his heart was heavy with the conviction that he was contributing in a big way to the destructive lifestyle of Dawson. God had tested him sorely over the last year and a half and now it was almost as though Riley was being brought full circle. Once again, he had to face how the choices he'd made as a godless young man still affected his life.

"I see no reason why we can't leave right away. Say, maybe in the next day or two. You do realize we may have to stay for some time? This isn't the kind of problem that's going to resolve itself overnight."

"I'll get us packed," Zandy stated, brushing aside his concern, and hurried off to coordinate the effort.

 za

The trip was set for the day following the next. They would take the stage and then the train. Zandy figured they'd be in Denver by the end of the week and then another day on the narrow-gauge mountain railroad before they'd finally reach Dawson. It was hard to imagine standing in her Missouri home one day, knowing that within a matter of just a few days, she would be hundreds of miles away in Colorado. Modern progress was a wonder!

Pamela was devastated by the news when Zandy came over to visit her at the Charbonneau house. Claudia kindly agreed to watch over their home while they were away, greatly relieving Zandy.

Pamela sat in silence, toying with a long blond braid. She thought longingly of how wonderful it would be to get away from her grandmother and the small-town life she'd come to hate. Then an even more attractive thought came to mind. *Zandy and Riley will have to pass through Kansas City to connect with their train*, she reasoned. *If only I could accompany them, perhaps I could get to Bradley.*

Waiting until Claudia had left the room for some trivial matter, Pamela quickly pushed her plan forward. "Zandy, could I accompany you to Colorado?"

Zandy was so shocked at Pamela's forward request that she could say nothing before Pamela continued.

"You know how I detest this town and, since my parents are determined to keep me separated from Bradley, why not add several hundred miles to that separation? I need desperately to get beyond these walls, and perhaps in Colorado I could forget about my heartache and start over."

"Colorado is hardly a solution to your broken heart," Zandy mused. "You would be more lonely than ever."

"I would have your friendship to get me through, and maybe you could introduce me to some of your old friends there."

Zandy had to smile at the remark. She had no friends in Dawson, save her family. In fact, the more she thought about how busy Riley would be with her father and how Ruth had their three-year-old daughter, Molly, to keep up with, the more Zandy thought it might be nice to have Pamela along for the company.

"I promise I won't be any trouble," Pamela said, taking Zandy's hand.

"I never thought you would be," Zandy replied. She wondered silently how she could talk Riley into allowing her to bring Pamela with them. "But how in the world would we convince your grandmother that such a trip would be in your best interest? After all, she'll no doubt miss you terribly."

Pamela smiled confidently. She'd broken through the first barrier of convincing Zandy that her company was needed. "*Grand-mère* will be happy for me to accompany you, especially if she knows that it will meet your needs."

Zandy scarcely realized the deception Pamela was pulling her into as Claudia rejoined them.

"*Grand-mère*, Zandy was just telling me that she longs for a traveling companion on their trip to Colorado. I have offered her my services, but we thought perhaps it would be wise to seek your approval on the matter." Pamela's conscience only bothered her a little that she'd actually told a lie.

Claudia narrowed her eyes slightly before turning to Zandy. "It is true that you wish Pamela to accompany you to Colorado?"

"I would very much enjoy her company," Zandy answered honestly. "I would, however, still need to approach my husband on the subject."

"I see," Claudia remained thoughtful for a moment, then turned to her granddaughter. "I believe it would be a good thing for you to travel. As I said when you first arrived, you've seen nothing of the world and perhaps with a better view of it, you won't pine away for that gold-digging dandy in Kansas City."

Pamela grimaced at her grandmother's reference to Bradley but then offered a sweet smile and nodded. "I know it would ease my suffering considerably."

"Very well," Claudia replied. "Alexandra, I'll have a draft prepared to pay for Pamela's ticket and travel needs."

And so it was settled, at least as far as Pamela was concerned. Zandy, however, knew she had a monumental task ahead in approaching Riley and winning him over to the idea.

৯

The next day, Riley, Zandy, and Pamela boarded the stage for Kansas City. Riley hadn't liked the idea of Pamela's joining them but, because his mind was so preoccupied with the problems in Colorado, he gave in easily, only telling Zandy that should any problem result from the matter it would be on her head. Zandy wanted to comment on her husband's words, but she was so relieved to have Riley's permission to bring Pamela that she let the issue drop.

Pamela was elated and in a better mood than Zandy or Riley had seen her since her arrival in town. She plotted in her mind, as the stage drew them closer to their train connection, how she would be reunited with Bradley. She vowed to see to it that they were married the very same day, before her parents could get wind of it and chase Bradley off again.

But Pamela's plans were not to be. A washed-out bridge made it necessary for the stage to detour, not once, but twice, and finally the road weary travelers picked up the train in Lawrence, Kansas, many miles west of Kansas City and Pamela's beloved Bradley.

Her mood changed dramatically as they pushed farther west, and Zandy thought she understood the real reason why. Riley found the ride irritatingly slow and took to pacing from car to car on a daily basis. It was during one of his strolls that he happened upon none other than Horace Tabor, the infamous Leadville Silver King and newly elected legislator from Colorado. He had added to his notoriety, Riley learned in conversation, by divorcing his wife and wedding his mistress, Baby Doe, in a hotel ceremony in Washington, D.C. They were on their way back to Denver, where they would set up housekeeping and start their new life together.

Tabor was a likeable enough man, with a drooping mustache and gray at the temples of his receding dark brown hair. His easygoing manner instantly put Riley at ease and, in talking, the men learned they had a great deal in common. Riley didn't return to the ladies until nearly two hours later, and it seemed that when he did his heart had been lightened considerably. Tabor had a real interest in the town of Dawson. Perhaps, Riley thought, he would offer them a way out of the dirty game of mining towns and outlaw gangs.

Pamela's sullen spirits could do nothing to spoil Zandy's excitement as the train pulled into Dawson, Colorado. She hadn't seen her family in over a year, and suddenly it seemed the most important thing in the world.

"Look, Riley," she exclaimed leaning across him. "There's Father and Ruth!"

Pamela followed Riley and Zandy from the train to the loading platform and waited grimly while Zandy fussed over each of her family members.

"I can't believe how Molly's grown," Zandy said of her little sister. "She was just a baby when I left Dawson. And just look at you," she said, turning to her thirteen-year-old brother. "Why, Joshua, you're nearly a man." This caused the boy to swell with pride. In spite of his younger brothers' laughter, he felt Zandy had bestowed a high honor upon him.

Eleven-year-old Bart and nine-year-old Samuel took hold of either side of Zandy's wrinkled traveling dress and began tugging on her skirts.

"Guess what, Zandy," Bart began.

"We had a bank robbery," Samuel finished for his brother.

Zandy cast a worried glance at her father, while Riley barely caught the words as he returned with their bags.

"What's this about a bank robbery?" he asked, coming alongside his wife.

"It's true," seven-year-old George exclaimed. "Those bad men rode into town, just big as you please."

Zandy had to suppress a smile at the little boy's recitation. Her heart had always held a soft spot for George, as he had been the baby for four years before Molly's arrival.

"George has that right," Burley stated. "But they only

managed to get away with several thousand dollars instead of the hundreds of thousands that had been there the day before. We had just decided at the last minute to send the money out on an early train to Denver, and it's a good thing we did."

"God was looking over us once again," Ruth added. Molly began fussing at all the ruckus and attention, so Ruth motioned them to join her. "Let's get out of the cold and head home for something warm to eat. I would imagine you all could use a good rest before we have much more conversation."

The mountains around Dawson reminded Pamela of prison walls. The rocky boulders jutted out in a mocking face that seemed to proclaim the isolation of the small Colorado town. She had never before seen such wonders, but she would gladly have turned her back on the beauty in order to return to Kansas City on the next available train.

She had remained so quietly fixed in the background that Zandy had nearly forgotten her. Noticing her blank stare as she surveyed the town around them, Zandy quickly reached out to pull Pamela into the circle of family.

"This is Pamela Charbonneau," Zandy introduced. "She's a good friend of Riley's and mine, and I invited her to come along with us. I hope you don't mind the fact that we didn't let you know ahead of time that she'd be joining us, but we were so anxious to get here."

"Any friend of yours is welcome," Ruth said, shifting Molly in order to shake Pamela's hand. "We're pleased to have you. Fact is, it's Riley and Zandy's house anyway. We just take up space there and do our best to keep things running smoothly."

"Don't let her fool you," Riley said with a grin. "This

woman is pure organized energy. If you don't believe me, just ask her husband." Everyone, including Ruth, laughed at this, while Pamela forced a weak smile to her lips.

"I'm pleased to meet you," she murmured and followed the entourage to their waiting carriages.

❧

Pamela was still miserable even after soaking in a hot bath and eating a hearty meal of the most succulent roast pork she'd ever tasted. She found herself in the company of Zandy and Ruth after the children had been dismissed to play. The housekeeper came and whisked Molly off for a nap, leaving the women to catch up on all the latest news.

"I knew Riley and Burley would be office-bound the minute you got here," Ruth began. She poured tea for Zandy and Pamela before sitting down to her own cup.

"So did I," Zandy remarked. "That was one of the reasons I was glad for Pamela's company. This whole town mess has Riley completely consumed. His spirit is bothering him something fierce, and I know that God is trying to help him put it all in order."

"Riley has certainly changed," Ruth said, then glanced hesitantly at Pamela.

"Oh, Pamela knows all about Riley," Zandy assured her stepmother. "In fact, it was Riley's coming to God that gave Pamela the courage to take the same step."

"Truly?" Ruth questioned, rather surprised.

Pamela ventured into the conversation only half-heartedly. "Yes. I felt moved by the things Zandy told me."

"Pamela is having a most difficult time," Zandy went on. "She had hoped to marry her young man in Kansas City, but her parents are rather overprotective and separated the two. They fear he's just after Pamela's inheritance."

"But it isn't true," Pamela jumped in. "Bradley would never do such a thing. He loves me."

Ruth smiled sympathetically. "I'm sure he does, but you must bear with your parents. We tend to fret and worry over our children, hoping and praying for the very best. I'm sure your mother is no different."

"My mother is a snob, Mrs. Stewart," Pamela promptly answered. "She is only concerned with what the Kansas City newspapers will say the morning after."

Ruth was taken aback by the young girl's bitter words, and Zandy tried to smooth the matter over. "I'm sure I'll be just as protective when my baby comes."

"What?" Ruth questioned. Her eyes widened in surprise. "Are you telling me what I think you are?"

Zandy smiled and nodded enthusiastically. "Yes! I'm going to have a baby in September."

"Oh, Zandy!" Ruth exclaimed and set aside her tea to embrace the younger woman. "How marvelous. What did Riley say?"

"Well, the fact of the matter is, I haven't told him. I was afraid he wouldn't let me take the trip if he knew."

Pamela felt an aching build in her heart. She could be married and having Bradley's children if only her parents hadn't interfered.

"You shouldn't keep things from him Zandy. He is your husband and in accordance with the Bible, you are subject to his authority," Ruth admonished.

Zandy winced. If only her stepmother knew how difficult coming under Riley's authority had been. She dearly loved her husband, but she'd been a Christian so much longer than he had that in some ways she felt that she knew better than he did on certain matters.

"I'll tell him tonight," Zandy promised.

"I have a headache," Pamela said suddenly. "Would you mind terribly if I retired for a nap?"

"Not at all, my dear," Ruth answered. "Do you remember the way to your room?"

Pamela nodded. "I'm sure I do. Thank you for the wonderful meal. And Zandy," she said turning to her friend, "congratulations."

Zandy beamed in happiness, making Pamela feel even more alienated. The room was smothering her with the joy of the two women, and Pamela hurried for the door, closing it firmly behind her. Leaning there against the heavy oak frame, Pamela felt the first tears flood her eyes. She ran for the stairs and the sanctuary of her room before anyone could stop her and ask what was wrong.

*

That evening in front of her dressing table, Zandy began the long process of pulling out hairpins and letting down her chestnut brown hair. She brushed in long, even strokes, while thinking of how she would share her news with Riley. He might be very angry with her for not telling him sooner, or he might be so overjoyed at the news that he'd completely forget the little matter of timing. Either way, she didn't hear him come into the room until he stood directly behind her.

Leaning down, Riley placed a kiss on her cheek. "You're mighty deep in thought, Mrs. Dawson."

Zandy put the brush down and rose to embrace her husband. "That I am," she murmured against his chest.

"I'm sorry I took so long, but I've a feeling you'll see a whole lot less of me before it gets any better. I guess I'm kind of glad you brought Pamela with you."

Zandy pulled away. "You truly are?"

"Yes," Riley smiled down at his wife. "You were smart to bring her, and I was wrong to hesitate. I'm sorry. Do you forgive me?"

Zandy swallowed hard. She felt more than a little guilty for keeping the news of the baby from him. "Only if you forgive me."

"Forgive you? For what?"

"Come sit down," Zandy said, pulling Riley to the edge of the bed.

"If I need to sit down, it must be something big," Riley said, looking deep into Zandy's eyes. "Better come clean quickly, Mrs. Dawson."

Zandy sat down beside Riley and folded her hands in her lap. "I'm going to have a baby."

"What!" Riley jumped to his feet. "Are you sure?"

Zandy couldn't even look him in the eye. "Yes, I'm sure and there's more."

Riley laughed. "A baby! Well, I'll be. I'm going to be a father! When did you find out?"

"That's what I need to talk to you about," Zandy said softly.

Riley immediately noted her sobriety and sat back down beside her. "What is it?"

"I knew about the baby before we left on this trip," Zandy said slowly. "I was afraid if I told you, you might not let me come along. I know it was wrong, and I'm sorry."

"Don't you trust me, Zandy?"

Her head snapped up, and she gazed into his brown-black eyes. "With my life!" she declared.

"But not with the life of our child?" His words hit her hard.

"It was just that I wanted so much to see my father and Ruth and the kids. I was afraid with the way you worry over me that you'd put your foot down and demand that I stay in Missouri and, Riley, I just couldn't bear that."

"So you decided how I would react before you gave me a chance to have any say in the matter?" Riley questioned.

"Well, you can be rather stubborn," Zandy said with a weak smile.

"Me? Take a look in the mirror, Mrs. Dawson, and let's discuss stubborn streaks."

"All right. I've admitted I was wrong."

"Yes, you were," Riley said firmly.

Zandy eased into his arms and snuggled against his neck. "But you forgive me, right?"

Riley laughed and wrapped his arms around her. "I forgive you, but please promise me you'll give me a chance next time. This is some kind of news and, if you'd only told me, I could have made arrangements for you to have an easier trip out here."

"I promise to trust you in the future," Zandy answered, feeling contentment replace her guilt.

"Good," Riley replied. "Now, when is my son due to arrive?"

four

The weeks moved slowly, one into the other, without Pamela so much as realizing that the harsh cold of winter was passing into a colorful display of mountain spring. The gardens outside the Dawson mansion had been carefully cultivated by Ruth Stewart and, in spite of the fact that Molly did her best to pick everything in sight, there grew an enchanting array of flowers and vegetation.

Pamela was bored, however. Bored and miserable. The snowcapped mountains surrounding Dawson did little to lift her spirits. She continued to pine for Bradley and spent most of every waking hour concentrating on her memories of their time in Kansas City.

Zandy and Ruth laughed and talked about the baby to come. At one point, they went into town to shop, and Pamela tagged along, wishing that she might find something to interest herself. It was hope ill-spent, as far as Pamela was concerned. She couldn't achieve the same spirit of light-heartedness as Zandy and Ruth. They were content to pick out material and plan baby clothes, while Pamela had nothing but her broken dreams.

Catching sight of a newly placed photography studio, Pamela talked Zandy into allowing her to sit for a photograph. Pamela wanted very much to mail the picture to Bradley, hoping that it would remind him of how much she loved him. Zandy reluctantly agreed to the picture and promised she'd think about whether or not it would be wise to mail the photo to Bradley.

Zandy continued to try to reason with Pamela. She shared Scripture after Scripture about God's desire that His children be blessed and happy. She quoted Psalms and Proverbs until she was breathless, all in hopes of pointing Pamela to the same faith that Zandy held in her own heart.

"Pamela, Proverb seventeen, twenty-two is just the verse for you," Zandy said one evening while sewing a tiny blanket. "I found it just the other day while I was having my devotions."

Pamela stared curiously but said nothing.

"Anyway," Zandy continued, "It says, 'A merry heart doeth good like a medicine: but a broken spirit drieth the bones.'"

"I have nothing to be merry about, Zandy." The words were given matter-of-factly, and Pamela offered nothing more on the matter.

Zandy put aside her blanket and reached across the small table to where Pamela's hands were folded in idle frustration. "We don't always understand why God allows certain things to happen in our lives. I know I couldn't understand why I had to meet up with the likes of Riley Dawson when he first came to this town. But God sees the bigger picture, and we have to trust Him with it."

"But it is so hard," Pamela said with a heaviness that threatened to break into sobs.

"I know," Zandy said and gave her friend's hand a squeeze. "But just remember this, when Moses' mother put him into the basket and had his sister set him afloat in the Nile, God was already sending Pharaoh's daughter to the river bank."

"I don't think I understand," Pamela admitted.

"God was already planning ahead. He wants us in our living and desires to seek His will and way for our lives. Often, however, we choose another path, and God realizes, as a loving Father, that giving us our own way would be harmful. He gives us the freedom to choose, but He also intervenes to redirect because He knows we are only human. Maybe God realized that Bradley would only bring you heartache and grief. Maybe God has someone better for you. A Christian man who will love and honor you, as he loves and honors the Lord."

"I can't believe that God would be so cruel to me," Pamela said, jerking her hands away from Zandy. She got to her feet and smoothed back the loose pieces of blond hair that had pulled out of her stylish chignon. "I don't want another man, Christian or no. I want Bradley, and if I can't have him I'll have no one!"

With that, Pamela stormed out of the room and from the house. She had a full head of steam and an elongated step by the time she reached the Dawson gardens.

The sky had faded into deep purple twilight, and stars were already visible in the velvety folds. Pamela forced herself to slow down and rethink her words. Zandy hadn't meant any harm, and Pamela knew that full well.

"Oh, Bradley," she whispered against the night skies. Just then someone grabbed her from behind, and Pamela felt steel-like arms pull her tight, while a leather-gloved hand fell across her mouth.

"Don't cry out," the hoarse voice sounded. "I've come to rescue you."

Pamela was nearly beside herself with joy. Bradley had come for her! She tried to turn and speak, but the arms held her tight.

"No, just stay quiet. I'll explain everything later. Just remember, this is for your own good. Now, do what I say."

Pamela nodded mutely, and the hand dropped from her mouth. The man pulled her backwards through the garden to an awaiting horse. Ominous black shadows kept Pamela from getting a good look at the man, but in her heart she was content to believe it was Bradley. After all, he had said he was there to rescue her. An ordinary kidnapper would never say such a thing.

The man hoisted her into the saddle of his horse, coming up behind her at the same time. Pamela settled into the seat and leaned back against the warmth of the man's chest. *Yes*, she thought to herself, *this is my Bradley, and he's come to take me home.*

They rode for hours, sometimes at a steady pace along the well-worn mountain road and other times more slowly, in order to avoid disaster in the pitch black that had become night. Eventually, the rhythmic ride caused Pamela to lose her grip on the saddle horn and fade into a weary sleep. She was safe and warm in the arms of the man she loved. What more could she want?

Pamela dreamed of Bradley's gallant rescue even as she slept. She saw herself laughing at how they'd fooled everyone and escaped the tyrannical rule of her parents. Bradley was gallant and dashing, and Pamela was happier than she'd thought possible. Bradley had saved her from loneliness, and that was all she knew.

The wind picked up and roared down through the tall ponderosa pines, giving a moaning cry that woke Pamela from her happiness. Stretching a bit, Pamela suddenly realized that she was no longer on the back of the horse. Opening her eyes, she was greeted with a warm, crackling fire and the unmistakable aroma of coffee.

Pamela sat up and rubbed the sleep from her face, and that was when she saw it. Two harsh, angry, unyielding eyes, glowing across the fire from her. The man who stared back at her was not Bradley! Nervously, Pamela scooted back a bit before demanding to know the man's identity.

"Who are you? Where's Bradley?" she asked as forcefully as she could.

The man did nothing for a minute. He just kept staring at her with eyes that would yield nothing more than something that closely resembled hatred. His lean, angular jaw was clenched tightly, so tightly in fact that Pamela could see a noticeable ticking in his cheek.

"Well?" she pressed for an answer.

"I might ask you the same," the deep voice sounded from across the flames.

"I presumed you knew. Didn't you help Bradley rescue me?" Pamela asked innocently.

"I don't know what you're talking about, lady." The man sprung to his feet like a circus cat performing its paces. Pamela shrank away. Her heart was beating wildly. Who was this man?

"I'm talking about this," Pamela finally offered in a weak voice. She waved her arm across the sky. "My rescue."

"I didn't plan to rescue you. I don't know who this Bradley is, and I sure don't know who you are." He came to stand no more than a foot or so away from her before he crouched down. "Who are you?"

Pamela began to tremble so hard that it was instantly noticeable to the man. He grumbled beneath his breath, walked to where his bedroll was, and brought back a blanket. Without any concern for the woman at his feet, he unrolled the blanket with a snap that ended in a cloud of dust.

"Here," he said and threw it down.

Pamela coughed and sputtered in the dirt cloud. Anger quickly replaced her fear, and Pamela got to her feet, casting the blanket to one side.

"How dare you!" she exclaimed and rushed at the surprised man. She pounded her fists against his chest while the stranger stood staring down at her in shocked wonder. Finally having had enough, he reached out in a flash and halted her assault.

"Who are you?" he asked in a whisper.

"I'm Pamela Charbonneau," her blue eyes flashed their anger, reminding the man of summer lightning.

A smile broke across his face for only a moment and then faded to a solemn line. "Why were you at the Dawson house?"

"I'm staying there with friends," she said and struggled to pull loose from his grip. "Or I should say, *was* staying there. Now that I've answered your questions, how about answering mine?"

The man shrugged and released her. "Jim," he said casually. "The name's Jim Williams."

"Should that mean anything to me?" Pamela asked stepping backwards several steps. She felt better putting the distance between them.

"Not unless Zandy told you about me," he replied.

"Zandy? Why would she know a ruthless outlaw like you?"

Jim laughed. "Outlaw, eh? I guess you would think that."

Pamela didn't care that the anger was fading from his face. "I demand that you tell me what's going on. I want to know now!" she screeched and stomped her foot.

Jim stared in wonder. Long ago, he had cared for Zandy Stewart, and just as long ago, he'd accused her of being less than pure in her actions with his boss, one Riley Dawson. It had taken some time for him to come back to Dawson, Colorado. When he did, however, he heard of how Zandy had been wrongfully accused of questionable behavior and how Riley had forced her into a loveless marriage. Since then, to save her had been his only intent. He would rescue her from a loveless, corrupt marriage. Instead, Jim had taken the wrong woman, and now she ranted and raved to know why an injustice had been done to her.

"I mean it!" Pamela's voice was rising to a shout. "I want to know why you took me. I want to know when you are going to release me. I want to know why—"

Pamela stopped as Jim turned to walk away. "Where are you going?"

Jim kept walking and Pamela ran after him, grabbing his arm. "You don't mean to leave me here alone, do you?"

Jim stopped and stared down at the youthful face. He suddenly felt very old and very troubled. "I have to think," he declared. "And, I can't do that with you caterwauling. Sit by the fire and you'll be fine. I'll be back when my head is clear."

With that, he pulled his arm loose and disappeared into the darkness. Pamela whirled on her heel and stalked back to the fire. She was worried, frightened, and just plain mad. The arrogance of the man left her shaking with rage. The memory of his piercing brown eyes left her trembling for other reasons.

Grabbing the blanket he'd thrown down, Pamela pulled

it around her and sat down. The trees rustled a haunting melody. Night sounds she'd not heard before became audible in her solitude. Pamela had never really been alone before. All of her life, there had been someone to watch over her or to do for her. Now there was no one, not even the angry man who'd taken her.

Tears came to Pamela's eyes as the distant scream of a mountain lion rang out. She pulled her knees to her chest and hugged the blanket close, pulling it over her head.

"God," she prayed, "please help me."

five

All his life, Jim Williams had only one desire. That was to get his own piece of the world and make something of himself. Now, at twenty-six, he was beginning to wonder if that day would ever come.

Even though the night air bore an unmistakable chill from the high-country snows, Jim felt a bead of sweat form on his forehead. He'd taken the wrong woman! To Zandy he could have explained that it wasn't kidnapping. He'd meant no harm and had only the best of intentions, but how could he tell this to the angry young woman who sat at his fire?

There was no answer in the wind as it blew across his face. There was no reasoning the matter away. When he'd first given thought to the plan of taking Zandy, he'd stopped thinking once he got past the taking part. He'd not even given himself a reasonable plan of action for how they might disentangle themselves from Riley Dawson's wrath once he realized his wife was gone.

Grimacing, Jim kicked at a fallen pine log. "Poor Zandy," he thought aloud. "I sentenced her to a life of misery, and all because I chose to believe what everyone was saying about her."

His memory reminded him that he had seen her leave Riley's house before dawn. That was the morning after Zandy's father had suffered injury in a mining accident.

Jim had presumed that Zandy had spent the night with Riley after fetching the doctor for her father. It wasn't until just recently he'd learned from one of his old buddies that Riley had actually drugged Zandy with the intention of ruining her reputation once and for all. A low growl escaped him as he relived the moment Pat Folkes had informed him of the truth.

He was too late to take back the time Zandy had been forced to spend as Riley's wife, but he'd hoped that he could rectify his angry dismissal and betrayal of their friendship by rescuing her now. But now he had some other woman in his care. A very beautiful woman named Pamela Charbonneau, with dark blue eyes that flashed electrically when she was mad.

With a heavy sigh, Jim made his way back to camp. There was nothing to do but apologize and take her back. Hopefully, she'd understand and get over it before they reached Dawson. Jim had no desire to have to answer to the law for his ill-planned scheme.

He reentered the camp silently and came upon Pamela from behind. She heard a muffled sound and turned, fearfully expecting to find a wild beast bearing down upon her. Seeing it was only Jim, Pamela hid her relief by pulling the blanket down tight around her face.

Jim felt at a loss for words as he took a seat on the ground, opposite Pamela. He waited, hoping that she might say something, but when she continued to ignore him, Jim finally spoke.

"Look, I'm sorry for taking you. I hadn't planned it that way. I thought you were Zandy. I just wanted to rescue her." He was trying to offer the most sincere apology he could, but the young woman refused to give him even the slightest consideration.

"Did you hear me?" Jim questioned, irritation edging his

voice. He fought for self-control in the face of her silence.

"Look, I don't know what you want me to say that I haven't already said. I'll take you back at first light, but for now we're stuck here."

Pamela kept her face hidden and remained silent, leaving Jim infuriated.

"All right," he said in complete exasperation. "If that's the way you want it, that's the way it'll be." He sauntered over to his saddle and dragged out the rest of his bedroll before plopping down on the ground.

"Remember what I said. We'll leave here at first light, so you'd better get some sleep."

Pamela had been determined to say nothing to him and, in her mind, she'd won her little part of the game. Now, however, her determination to remain awake failed. She gradually leaned herself over, until finally she lay in a curled ball just beyond the fire. Her back was warmed by the dying flames, while her front felt the icy wind bite into her skin. Nevertheless, Pamela slipped into a troubled sleep. In her waking moments, she knew she'd be grateful when dawn finally arrived.

&

In the early morning light, Jim stared down at the childlike woman. Her blond hair had come undone and spilled out from the blanket like a veil. The blanket itself had slipped down far enough to reveal her delicate face in sleep. She had long pale lashes and a pert, almost tiny mouth that Jim remembered, with a shudder, could let go with a most impressive assault of words.

Kneeling down beside her, Jim was struck for a moment by Pamela's seeming frailty. She was so small, he thought. Petite by the standards of most women. How could he have thought she was Zandy? Zandy was at least a head taller and her hair was dark, not golden like ripening grain.

Jim shook head. What was he doing? Reaching over, he gently shook her shoulder.

"Go away," she muttered and rolled to her other side. The blanket fell away revealing her disheveled state. Her once white blouse was now dirt stained and pulled out from the waist of her tailored burgundy skirt. The skirt itself had ridden up to give Jim a view of silken ankles and dainty satin slippers.

Now he was really disturbed. Seeking to rid himself of his attraction to her, Jim gave Pamela's arm a firm smack and jumped back.

"What are you doing?" Pamela exclaimed, coming up from the ground. She got to her feet and whirled around to face her attacker. "Are you now going to beat me?"

Jim laughed. "At least you're talking to me. Come on. I've got breakfast ready, and we'll be riding out of here in about fifteen minutes."

Pamela put her nose in the air and turned away. "I shan't eat anything you provide." She moved away with a regal step that was almost amusing, given her state of disarray.

"My grub is the only grub here," Jim said with a shrug of his shoulders. "Suit yourself, but it's going to take us most of the day to get back to Dawson."

Pamela seemed to come wide awake at once. "Are we really so far away?" She had thought their ride only a short one.

"We rode for over eight hours. Even if the pace wasn't always very fast," Jim admitted, "it was steady."

Pamela frowned, then noticed her hair. "Oh my," she murmured. "My hair!"

Jim grinned. "Looks fine. I'm just sorry my blanket got you so dirty."

Pamela hadn't noticed the stains on her clothes, nor the way her blouse hung outside her skirt. A gasp escaped her lips as she fought to put everything aright at the same time.

Jim chuckled and walked over to where the coffee steamed aromatically from a worn pot. "Coffee?"

Pamela shook her head vigorously. "I prefer tea, but I suppose you don't have any."

"No, you got that right," Jim replied. "I do have cold biscuits and jerked beef. I know you're used to better, but it's filling." Reluctantly, she gave in and, after combing her fingers through her hair, joined Jim.

Pamela ate silently while Jim watched her for a moment. In spite of her desire for tea, she eventually took a cup of coffee in order to wash down the biscuit and felt grateful for the warmth of the liquid in her stomach.

Jim could stand the silence no more. He pressed forward to ease his curiosity by asking her questions. "Why did you come so willingly with me? Why didn't you fight?"

Pamela no longer felt angry with Jim. Now she just wanted to get back to Dawson and Zandy's care. "I thought," she finally answered, "that you were someone else."

"That's right," Jim remembered. "You kept mentioning some other guy. Bradley, wasn't it?"

Pamela nodded. "Yes. Bradley Rayburn, the man I love."

Jim digested the information for a moment. "Is he your intended?"

"I hope so," Pamela said and in her voice was the misery that came from the weeks—months—of separation. "It's been so long since we've been together, he may well have forgotten me by now."

"A man would have a difficult time doing that," Jim mused aloud.

Pamela gave him a quizzical look, then continued. "My parents separated us. I thought perhaps Bradley had come to take me away. When you said you'd come to rescue me, what else was I to think?"

"So you just climbed on the first horse offered, mindless of the danger and stormed off into the night?"

Pamela glared at Jim and narrowed her eyes. Again Jim noticed how blue they were. "I thought you were Bradley! I wanted you to be," she added in a wistful voice.

"Well, I guess I can sympathize with that," Jim answered. Seeing that Pamela had finished her fare and that the sun was even now peeking up over the snowy eastern range, Jim started collecting his things. "We'd best be on our way."

Pamela stood uncomfortably and frowned. "I would like a moment of privacy," she murmured.

Jim immediately understood and nodded. "I'll saddle the horse and stow this gear."

Pamela watched him move away, totally unconcerned with her urgent need. She looked first in one direction and then another, somewhat bewildered by her predicament. Jim glanced up and realized she'd probably never had to see to nature's call in the great outdoors.

"Just pick a direction," he called over his shoulder. "One way is just about the same as another."

Pamela reddened and stalked off toward a thicket of brush. She could hear Jim chuckling in the background, and it irritated her more than she could say.

"We'll see how he laughs when we get back to Dawson," she muttered.

The mountain trail was winding and laborious for the horse. He struggled against the weight of two passengers for, while Pamela barely weighed a hundred pounds, Jim was a good-sized portion of baggage. From time to time, he dismounted and led the horse while Pamela rode alone. All the while, Jim kept thinking about what he'd done and how he'd explain himself in Dawson.

For the first time, Pamela began to notice the scenery. The land around her was both beautiful and deadly. At times, the roadway was barely suited to accept the width of a horse, and Pamela felt herself leaning toward the rocky wall as loose gravel and rock shifted and plummeted down the ravine.

A heavy cloud bank moved in and rained on the valleys below them. Pamela watched as it blanketed everything in billowy blackness and lingered on as the morning passed into afternoon.

When they stopped to rest the horse and eat a meager lunch, Jim watched the skies, shaking his head. "It doesn't look good," he said.

"What doesn't look good?" Pamela asked curiously.

"It looks like we're going to get wet," he replied and motioned behind her. "There's another storm moving in."

Pamela glanced at the heavy sky and shrugged. At least she'd be back with Zandy and Riley by nightfall. Thinking of Zandy, Pamela remembered Jim's words from the night before.

"Why did you want to take Zandy?" she suddenly questioned. "I mean, why did you think she needed rescuing?"

Jim pulled his hat down low before shoving his hands into his jeans. "I wronged her a long time ago," he finally said. "I was partially to blame for her ending up in a loveless marriage with that no-good Riley Dawson."

Pamela nearly choked on her food. "Loveless marriage?" She began to laugh gaily. "There were never two people more in love than Riley and Zandy. She worships the ground he walks on. He stares at her with such devotion that I honestly think he'd perish if she were taken from him."

Jim's eyes narrowed and his face grew flushed. "I don't believe you!"

Pamela got to her feet and smoothed her burgundy skirt into place. "Well, it doesn't much matter what you believe. It's true. Zandy and Riley are very happy. In fact, they're going to have a baby in the autumn."

Jim moved away angrily. He threw things back into his saddlebags, muttering all the while. "No one could be happy with Riley Dawson."

"But Zandy is," Pamela said, refusing to give an inch on the argument. "Riley has changed from the man he used to be."

"What would you know of the man he used to be?" Jim raged. "I knew him then. I worked for him and he was a cutthroat, no-good person who...." His words faded into a growl. "He was just ruthless, that's all."

"He got saved," Pamela offered. "Zandy says God made Riley a new man, and she loves him."

"I can't believe this trash," Jim said, throwing the reins over the horse's neck. "Get up there," he said, motioning to the saddle.

"I will not be ordered about. You're just mad because the woman whom you thought needed you, doesn't. You should have checked things out a little better."

"Get over here so I can help you into the saddle," Jim

muttered between clenched teeth. Pamela's news just couldn't be true. Surely he hadn't been even more stupid than he'd already figured.

"I won't," Pamela said, striking a pose with hands on hips.

"Suit yourself," Jim replied and swung up into the saddle. "You can walk for a while." He nudged the horse forward and didn't even look back to see if Pamela followed him.

She did, though. She was angry at Jim for refusing to apologize for his temper and even angrier at herself for losing her ride. She grimaced at each step, feeling the sharp rocks as they cut into her thin-soled slippers. Then the rain began to fall.

First it only misted, making everything damp and cold. Then it fell in earnest, with huge drops that saturated everything in its path. Pamela struggled to keep pace with the horse and finally could take no more. Crumbling to the ground, she panted in exhaustion, near to tears for her folly.

Having cooled down considerably, Jim managed to keep a backward glance on Pamela. It would do her good, he thought, to break a bit of that willful, mean-spiritedness. But, when he saw her fall to her knees, he felt guilty for his own meanness and returned to where she sat.

Without a word, Jim got down from the horse, lifted Pamela into his arms, and remounted. Neither one said a thing, and a silent truce was born.

six

The rain fell in such a deluge that returning the same way they'd departed from Dawson became impossible. Each mountain stream was rising rapidly as the rains continued throughout the day. Finally, they came to a place where they could go no farther.

"We'll have to wait it out. By morning it should go down. This is just a cloudburst," Jim said, hoping against hope that he was right. "If not, we'll go back a ways and pick up another trail."

Pamela nodded. She was weary and cold and hungry. Nothing could have pleased her more than a warm bed and supper but, next to that dream, getting off the horse was second best.

Jim took a small hatchet and cut branches from the pines to form a shelter. It wasn't much, but it kept a good deal of the water off of them. Eventually, the rain seemed to pass on down the valley and, though the sun didn't come out to warm things, it was a relief.

Pamela succumbed to her exhaustion and fell into a deep sleep. She was mindless of the cold and hunger, as well as the dark brown eyes that watched her with a strange interest. When she awoke it was morning again, and she was stunned to realize she was alone.

"Jim!" she called, crawling out of the lean-to. "Jim!" Her voice held a frantic tone. She hadn't realized until that moment that she'd come to depend on the stranger for her own security.

"I'm here," Jim called, coming from a heavy growth of small pines. "I was catching us some breakfast." He held out a couple of ground squirrels and laughed at Pamela's wrinkled-up nose.

"You'll think they're grand once I get them cooked and you sink your teeth into them."

Pamela rolled her eyes. "I can't imagine feeling that way." But her stomach growled loudly, causing Jim to laugh even more.

Embarrassed, Pamela excused herself to some privacy and didn't return until Jim had the monstrous little things skinned and spitted over a small fire.

"Where did you get dry wood?" she asked, taking her seat beside the fire.

"You just have to know where to look," Jim said with grin. "The forest is filled with all sorts of wonders, if you know where to find them." With that, he pulled a handful of berries from his vest pocket.

"How marvelous!" Pamela exclaimed, and reached out to take some of the berries. She didn't concern herself with whether they were dirty or clean and popped them into her mouth with a smile. "Oh, they're wonderful."

Jim thought her most attractive when she smiled. "How old are you?" he asked without thinking.

"Eighteen," she said in surprise. "Why?"

"I just wondered. You look so young, almost like a child." He saw her frown and waved it off. "No offense."

Pamela relaxed a bit and nodded. "I understand."

"I really am sorry," Jim continued. "I feel bad for all I've put you through, and I guess," he paused, trying to think of how to word his thoughts, "I just don't want you to be mad at me. I honestly meant you no harm. I'm not the kind of man who goes around taking women on a regular basis."

Pamela laughed, "I'm sure you don't."

It was the only reply she felt comfortable in making. In truth, she was beginning to notice things about Jim that she hadn't before. Like the way he made her feel secure. That had completely surprised her.

She watched him work at cooking the food, turning it until it was golden and brown. She accepted one of the sticks of meat and looked up questioningly.

"I promise, it won't be as bad as you think. Eat it with this," he said and handed her a biscuit. "I brought quite a few of these with me."

Pamela did as he instructed her and found that the taste was bearable. Her hunger appeased, she got up to stretch and walk out the soreness in her back and legs.

Jim was putting things away and dousing the fire when she returned. For a moment, Pamela found herself thinking of his apology and the sincere way his eyes had met hers. He wasn't the ruthless outlaw she'd originally considered him. No, he was just a misguided soul, pining for a love that could not be. Just like she was. The thought shocked Pamela and her head snapped up to find Jim's warm brown eyes watching her.

"Ready?" he asked.

"Yes, I suppose," she said with a glance at the horse. "Although I'm not thinking overly kind thoughts of the ride ahead."

"Better than walking all the way," Jim mused and Pamela heartily agreed.

The horse picked his way down the muddy, rock-strewn

path. This trail was not as well developed as the one they'd used before, but the rain-swollen creeks prevented them from crossing to the better one so they had to make do with what lay before them.

Pamela found the aching in her back more than she could bear and finally gave in and leaned against Jim. He didn't seem to mind, and she tried to forget the impropriety of the entire matter, reminding herself that the last two days had been filled with improprieties.

"We'll stop and water the horse," Jim said, sliding over the animal's rump. "We're making good time in spite of the rain and flooding. We'll probably be back to Dawson before dark."

"It can't be soon enough," Pamela remarked, letting Jim lift her from the horse's back.

When he set her down, she remained fixed for a moment, looking up into his eyes. Then the screech of jaybird broke her thoughts, and she moved away to let him work with the horse.

Jim led the animal to the rapidly moving stream and allowed him to drink his fill. With a nervous snort, the gelding lifted his head and flattened his ears. Something was setting the horse on edge.

Jim glanced around, wondering if a bear or mountain lion was nearby. He lifted his eyes to the rocky ledges overhead but, seeing nothing, tried to pull the horse back with him to where Pamela waited.

The gelding whinnied and pulled away, rearing slightly and pounding the damp earth with its powerful hooves.

"What's wrong?" Pamela questioned, then her eyes grew wide and Jim saw her mouth open as if to say something more.

A sharp blow landed on the back of his head, and Jim instantly lost consciousness, slumping to the dirt. The horse reared, slamming its hooves down inches from Jim's face before charging away from the scene.

Pamela stared at the three men who faced her. They were leering and ugly and frightfully filthy. She backed away a step or two, not wanting to leave Jim to their mercy, yet knowing that if they caught up with her, her own fate could be worse than death.

She turned to run and managed to get several yards away before the youngest of the three caught up with her and threw her roughly over his shoulder.

"See if that fool has anything of value on him," the man yelled. "I'm taking her with us. Ma will know what to do with her."

"I know what to do with her, Joe," one of the others called back. This drew laughter from all three and left Pamela with a sickening feeling in the pit of her stomach.

The stench of the man rose up to assault her nose. Though she was more than a little dirty herself, this man smelled of death and rot. She struggled against his hold, but he only tightened his grip and laughed.

"You might as well cooperate, missy. You ain't going nowhere." By this time, the other two had joined him and Pamela could see that they were appraising her intently.

"I'd say she's a proper lady," one of the men said, coming alongside her. Pamela could see that a long hideous scar marred his face. It cut a path across his nose and ended just above his lip.

"Now, Knifenose," the other one said, running his tongue over his large lips. "You ain't pretty enough to be courting a proper lady. Iffen she really is a proper lady, then you'd best leave her to me." They snorted laughs, leering and commenting, until finally they reached the place where their horses were tethered.

The man called Joe pulled Pamela from his shoulder and threw her across his horse. The saddle horn pounded like a knife into her ribs, and Pamela let out a cry.

"Keep quiet," the man said, taking a seat in the saddle. He pulled her across his lap, then urged his horse forward.

"Was he dead?" Joe asked Knifenose, and Pamela held her breath waiting for the answer.

"Will be soon enough," Knifenose replied. "He didn't have much of anything on him so I didn't figure he deserved to be eased out of his misery."

Pamela shuddered at their cruelty and felt herself grow faint.

Jim struggled against the blackness and cleared his vision only enough to see three men taking Pamela into the pines. He tried with all his might to get up, but the void filled his eyes once again, and he fell hard against the dirt.

"Pamela," he whispered.

seven

"Don't try to move, son," a deep voice was saying.

Jim opened his eyes and squinted against the light of day. A white-haired, bearded stranger came into view overhead.

"Who are you?" Jim asked, putting a hand to the painful throbbing on the side of his head.

"The name's Caleb Emerson," the man replied with a warm smile. "Look's like you've been bushwhacked. They robbed ya clean, took all your goods, and left ya for dead."

Jim moaned and tried to roll onto his side. "I have to go after them."

"Whoa there, fella," Caleb said, putting a strong arm out to restrain Jim's movement. "You took a nasty hit to the head. I stopped the bleeding, and it's not life threatening, but you're gonna have to rest a while."

"I can't," Jim said. He lifted his eyes to the sky. "They've taken more than my goods."

"Nothing worth your life," the man offered.

"Yes, I'm afraid there was." Jim remembered blue eyes and a face that was only beginning to smile in his presence. "I wasn't traveling alone," Jim finally said. "There was a woman with me."

"Your wife?" Caleb asked in a concerned tone.

"No," Jim said and fell back against the ground. "It's a terribly long story, but I'm afraid I am responsible for the young woman, and now I have to find her."

"Well, you ain't going anywhere just yet," Caleb said sympathetically. "Why don't you just rest for a spell and eat some grub? After that, maybe you'd best tell me the whole story."

Against his will, Jim ate a bit and slept a great deal. He didn't awaken again until midmorning the following day, but his head hurt less and his vision was clearer.

"What time is it?" he asked, struggling to sit.

Caleb gave him a hand before glancing up at the sky. "'Pears to be about eleven."

"What day is it?"

"Now that's a little more difficult," Caleb replied with a smile. "Best I can figure, it's Thursday."

"If that's true, then I've only lost a day," Jim said, thinking aloud and rubbing his head.

"You gonna tell me what's going on?" Caleb asked.

Jim nodded. "I will if you'll give me some more of that stew you fed me yesterday."

Caleb chuckled and pulled out a tin plate from his saddlebag. "Sure thing." He dished up the stew from where it warmed over a dying fire. "By the way, I've got some good news for you."

"You found her?" Jim asked hopefully.

"Not your lady friend," Caleb said, sorry to see the hope leave the young man's face. "But, I did find your horse."

"That is good news," Jim admitted. He'd need a mount if he was going to find Pamela.

Caleb waited until Jim had eaten his fill of the stew, then curiosity got the better of the old drifter. "Who are you, son? You and that young lady elopin'?"

Jim shook his head. "Nothing so honorable," he replied. "The name's Williams. Jim Williams." Jim held out his hand to take the stranger's. They shook firmly before Jim continued. "I made a big mistake. In fact, I made several. One mistake I acted out a long time ago, and the most recent came because I was trying to right that wrong."

"I think you just got me more confused than I was to begin with," Caleb said with a laugh.

Jim eased back against a small boulder and rested his head. "I thought a certain young lady, a friend of mine from the past, needed rescuing from a bad situation. I decided to sneak down to where she lived and take off with her. I thought I'd get her to safety and let her decide from there what she wanted to do. But, instead of the woman I planned to take, I ended up taking someone completely different. Someone I didn't even know, until just a few days ago."

"I see," Caleb said, without any emotion betraying how he felt on the matter.

Jim grimaced at the dull ache that haunted his thoughts. "She came willingly. Fact was, she thought I was someone else who'd come to rescue her."

"So this young woman needed saving, too?"

Jim laughed. "You could say that, I suppose. She thought she did. Fancied herself in love with some city slicker. She thought he'd come to save her in the dead of night and, because it was dark, she didn't know that I wasn't him. We rode through the night, and she fell asleep in my arms. I really thought I was doing a noble thing. When I stopped for a spell to rest the horse, I put her on the ground to sleep, and then I built a fire. That was when I realized she wasn't at all who I thought she was."

"What happened then?"

Jim looked down at his booted feet. "I got mad. I got real

mad, in fact. I couldn't believe I'd grabbed the wrong woman. When she woke up, she was mad. Scared, too, and who could blame her? Here she was, just a little bitty thing, and some big ol' brute of a man had dragged her off in the night. She ranted and raved at me, and those blue eyes of her flashed brighter than any summer lightning storm you've ever seen."

Caleb smiled at the reference. "My wife used to be the same way."

"You're married?" Jim asked, forgetting for a moment to continue with his story.

"Was," Caleb said with a sadness to his voice. "She passed on a few years back. I know I'll see her again someday, but I sure miss her now."

Jim didn't say a word.

"Now what about your little bitty gal? What happened after her rantin' and ravin'?"

"I'm afraid I stormed off and left her alone by the fire. I knew it was a mean thing to do. She was obviously not used to outdoor life, but I wanted to put her in her place. I had to think, too, and I couldn't do that with her yelling and screeching at me like a hoot owl on a wildcat's back."

Caleb laughed out loud at this. "Did your leavin' settle her down?"

"Yeah, and then some," Jim admitted. "She wouldn't even talk to me when I got back. But, the next day things kind of mended themselves. I apologized and explained myself and promised I'd get her back home safely. Now it appears I've caused her harm once again."

"Don't fret about it, son. You need to get well and then we'll go out after her."

"We?" Jim looked the older man in the eye.

"Sure," Caleb said with a nod. "I can't let you go out there all alone. Now, did you see who took your little bitty gal?"

"Her name's Pamela," Jim said, though he liked the nickname. "All I saw was a vague image of the man who ransacked my pockets. He had a hideous scar that ran over his nose and down to his lip."

"That'd be Knifenose McCoy," Caleb muttered under his breath.

"You know them?" Jim said, sitting up abruptly.

Caleb ran a hand through his rough white beard. "I've been drifting these here parts since my wife died. There's a gang of outlaws that goes down into Dawson on a regular basis and wreaks havoc on everybody. It's the Owens gang, headed up by the mother of two of the men. Old Knifenose McCoy has been riding with 'em for a while now. If it's them, then I've got a good idea where they've taken your gal."

"Then let's go!" Jim exclaimed and got unsteadily to his feet. His head pounded, but he was undaunted.

"Nah," Caleb said and reached out to pull Jim back down. "That old mama of theirs ain't gonna let anything happen to Little Bitty. She's a real smart one, that woman. She's cultured and the real brains behind most of their activities. You just rest and get your feet back under you steadylike, and we'll head over to their hideout tomorrow."

"We can't let her spend another night in their company," Jim said in complete exasperation. "Those men might...well, they could...." He couldn't even bring himself to say what might happen.

"You gotta trust the good Lord to look over her, Jim. Christianfolk know that He's got all the answers, and He's the one looking out over those who can't look out for themselves. That'd be your little bitty gal. We'll just pray about it and ask Him to mosey on over to where she's at and surround her with His angels. You know the Bible says in Psalm ninety-one, verse eleven that 'He shall give his angels charge over thee, to keep thee in all thy ways.'"

"You believe that, Caleb?" Jim asked wearily. He was giving in to the misery of his body and hated himself for doing so.

"You bet I believe it!" Caleb said enthusiastically. "Ain't you a Christian, Jim?"

Jim put a hand to his head and stretched his legs back out in front of him. "My ma and pa were both God-fearing people. They brought me up to respect the Word of God and to go to church on Sunday. I listened to Ma tell me Bible stories and, one day, when I was just a tike, she asked me if I wanted to go to heaven when I died. I said, sure. I mean, I figured it beat all out of going to the other place."

Caleb chuckled, "That's no lie."

"Anyway, I repeated a prayer she told me. When I was done, she explained how all a body had to do to get saved and go to heaven was to accept Jesus as their Savior. She told me that when I accepted Jesus and asked Him to forgive my sins, I became a new person."

"That's for sure, too!" Caleb agreed.

"Well, I figured she wasn't lying," Jim continued, "but, in truth, I never felt any different. I mean, I didn't go out of my way to do wrong, but I didn't feel exactly called to preach, either. I guess over the years I figured being a Christian and all just didn't take."

"Sinful critters have a hard way of looking at life," Caleb said softly. "They see the things they've done, and they know they're no good. God sees the things they've done, and knows there's a chance for them to do different. Satan comes along, though, and tells them that there isn't any other way, and that they're the most miserable excuses for human bein's that ever existed. Satan makes sure he stands planted between those struggling folks and God, just to block out the view. But it don't work that way for long."

"It don't?" Jim questioned.

"Nope," Caleb replied and leaned back. "God sends them angels to surround you. They beat back old Satan and tell him to mosey on out, 'cause this property has God's mark on it."

"And does he?" Jim asked. "Does Satan back off?"

"You bet he does. God looks after His own, I told you that, son."

"But what if I'm not His own? What if Pamela's not?"

"Everything is God's, Jim. The world and all that's in it. The people, the animals, the trees—it all belongs to Him. It's just that some folks don't reckon God is theirs."

Jim felt the need to lie down and stretched out beside the glowing embers. "So you think I belong to God, too?"

"I think you need to answer that one for yourself, son," Caleb replied. "Give God a chance. He's not likely to hold a grudge for your lack of understandin'. Just seek Him out, and ask His forgiveness. It's never too late to change the path you're on."

Jim closed his eyes, and a bit of peace began to trickle into his heart. "Sounds like good words to think on," he muttered before dozing off into a deep sleep.

eight

Pamela stared fearfully into the gray-blue eyes of an older woman. The woman was taller than Pamela by half a foot and had an athletic youth to her that led Pamela to believe she was perfectly able to hold her own in any situation.

"What's your name?" the woman demanded.

"I might ask you the same," Pamela said, lifting her chin defiantly.

The woman studied her for a moment, then gave a brief laugh. "You're a spunky one, just like the boys said." She paused, eyes narrowing. "But you'll learn that cooperating with me will get you a lot less aggravation. My name is Esther Owens. I run this group of ruffians, and I'm no dawdling fool to be taken advantage of. I'm Eastern-educated, and I know well the ways of this world, so it would be best if you got it into your head now that I'm fully capable of running this show."

Pamela stared openly at the woman. Her reddish brown hair had been carefully pulled back and neatly knotted at the nape of her neck. Her dark brown riding skirt and snug matching jacket showed off a still youthful figure. But it was Esther's eyes that held Pamela's attention. They were purposeful and firm, and, just as Esther had stated, they betrayed a look of intelligence that Pamela couldn't deny.

"My boys tell me they killed your man," Esther began again. "Do you have other family?"

Pamela still refused to speak. In truth, she wasn't sure

she could after Esther's reference to Jim's death. Pamela felt her hands trembling and clutched them tightly together to avoid giving herself away.

Esther shook her head. "I'll leave you to yourself for a time. Maybe staying in this hole will give you reason to talk to me." Without any other word on the matter, Esther pulled the heavy wood door closed, and Pamela heard the unmistakable sound of her barring it from the outside.

Now Pamela was truly scared. She'd been livid at the way Esther's "boys" had treated her. They seemed inclined to speak suggestively, reminding Pamela that she was under their complete control. But it was Esther's words about Jim that left Pamela void of hope. Jim was taking her home. He alone knew where and why she'd been removed from Dawson in the first place, and now he was gone.

Pamela looked around the dimly lit room. The place was hardly wider than her arm span and only about half again as long. The rough, plank walls had never seen a coat of paint and the floor was dirt. There was nothing but a filthy cot for furniture, and a six-inch slit in the wall overhead offered the only light.

"Oh, God," she thought aloud, "what do I do?"

Esther Owens looked down the table at her gang and shook her head. Two of those present were her own sons, the rest were drifters and renegades who'd learned of her business dealings and sought to join up.

The men argued among themselves over one thing or another while Esther waited for a heavyset woman to serve their lunch. The sound of several riders approaching brought instant quiet to the table. Esther got up quickly and crossed to the window.

"It's just the rest of the boys," she said, coming back to the men.

Several grunts confirmed they'd heard her speak before they launched into a new set of arguments. Esther tapped her fingers on the table, waiting for the new arrivals to join them. They would be bringing her supplies from Denver. Hopefully, they'd bring a newspaper or two, maybe even a book.

Several men burst through the door, two of them carrying wooden crates.

"Take those to my room," Esther instructed and got up to follow the men from the room. "The rest of you men finish your eating and get back to work. We've got a big job to pull tomorrow, and I don't want anything to go wrong," she called over her shoulder.

Silence fell across the table. Although she was just a woman, these men knew her mind to be the keenest they'd encountered. There wasn't a man, young or old, sitting there who didn't know just how much they needed Esther Owens.

Esther directed the men to place the crates on her bed. "Now get yourselves some food. I'll need to talk to you when you're finished." The men nodded and left the room, closing the door behind them.

Esther began sorting through the boxes. She smiled broadly as her hand came to the newspaper that lined the bottom of one of the crates. Pulling it out, she took herself over to her rocking chair and began to read.

The price of silver was climbing, as were railroad stocks. The Atchison, Topeka, & Santa Fe Railroad was advertising tracts of land to entice immigrants to come west and settle along the train routes. There was some speculation that the Santa Fe desired to place a route across the southern U.S. territories, all the way to the coast, but no one was taking that venture very seriously.

Esther read on, drinking in the news and realizing, as she did every time a newspaper came her way, that she missed big-city life and knowing what was happening as it happened. She was about to put the paper aside when a photograph caught her eye. Staring at it hard, Esther began to smile.

The story below the photograph told of a young woman who'd disappeared from Dawson, Colorado. The picture was unmistakably that of the woman who was now captive in her shed out back. Esther wanted to shout when she read that Pamela Charbonneau was a wealthy socialite from Kansas City. There was good money to be made in this, and Esther was already putting together the ransom note in her mind. Tossing the paper onto the bed, Esther made her way back to the shed. She would confront Pamela with her news and decide from there how they would address the issue of a ransom.

⁂

Pamela had tried every way possible to escape her prison. She'd pulled and pushed at the door, only to realize that it was a hopeless case. She'd checked the walls for any hint of weakness but, finding none, could only pace out her frustrations.

She remembered something Zandy had once told her about God. She'd said that God would never leave you and that, no matter what happened in your life, He would always hear you when you prayed. Glancing up at the sagging ceiling, Pamela wondered if it were true. Would God really hear her if she prayed?

"I guess it's worth trying," Pamela muttered, seeking to convince herself. She tried to remember just how Zandy started her prayers. "Father," she whispered, "Zandy told me I could pray and You would hear me. Well, I'm in quite a fix right now, and I could certainly stand to be heard. Fact is, I need a great deal of help, and I don't know where it might come from. God, nobody but You and these outlaws even know I'm here. Please help me to get away from these people. Help me to escape to safety. I promise I'll never be difficult again, if You will just answer this prayer. Amen.

"There," Pamela stated in complete resolve, "that's done." She waited a few minutes, not moving a muscle, as if to see how God would answer her request. The silence washed over her in waves, but nothing seemed changed or the slightest bit different.

"I wish I knew more about this Christian stuff," Pamela sighed aloud. "Does it happen right away? How do you know if God hears you?" Just then the sound of someone outside the door startled Pamela.

Esther Owens opened the door and with her came a flood of daylight. Pamela squinted her eyes and stepped back a pace.

"Well," Esther began with a strange smile, "I've just come upon a bit of news from Denver. It was rather fascinating, and I thought perhaps you would enjoy hearing about it. Would you?"

Pamela lowered her head and said nothing.

"I asked you a question, Miss Charbonneau."

Pamela's head snapped up at the name. Esther laughed heartily and leaned back against the wall.

"So, you are Pamela Charbonneau of Kansas City and lately of Dawson?"

"Yes," Pamela finally admitted.

"The article in the Denver paper stated that it was unknown as to whether you had been taken or had simply disappeared on your own. Which was it?" Esther questioned curiously.

"It's none of your concern," Pamela retorted in a defiant tone. "What do you plan to do with me?"

"Well, the article also said that you are from a very wealthy family. Don't you imagine your poor folks would pay well to see you returned safely?"

Pamela realized the woman meant business. "I suppose they might. However, we are rather estranged at the moment. I came to Dawson with friends and, in truth, those friends would probably pay a hefty reward to have me returned. After all, I was in their care." Pamela's mind was moving way ahead of her mouth. Returning to her parents would put her in Kansas City, but they'd no doubt just ship her off again. No, perhaps it would be better to go home to Zandy and Riley. Then maybe Zandy could make a plea to her parents for her return to Kansas City and her marriage to Bradley.

Pamela was still lost in selfish thought when Esther spoke again. "Who are these friends in Dawson?"

"Riley and Alexandra Dawson," Pamela stated matter-of-factly.

Esther's eyes widened a bit before she resumed her mask of sober indifference. "*The* Riley Dawson? The one who owns the town?"

"The very same," Pamela admitted, and folded her arms across her dirty blouse. "I was staying with them. Mrs.

Dawson is my dearest friend."

"Ummm," Esther said, letting the information soak in. Perhaps the girl was right. There might be a greater advantage to approaching the Dawsons versus trying to work with people hundreds of miles away in Kansas City.

"This bears consideration," Esther muttered. "It also means taking a little more care with you. I'm moving you up to the house. I'll keep you there and maybe even let you clean up. You'll cooperate with me though, or I'll move you right back here. Is that understood?"

Pamela nodded her head. She wasn't about to pass up the chance to move from the shack. Wherever she was going would surely present a better chance at escape than this place.

"Good," Esther said and took hold of Pamela's arm. "Don't think to try anything. We're located in a box canyon so there's basically only one way out. The walls around us are jagged granite, more than one hundred feet straight up. Beyond those are the harshest mountain wastelands you would ever want to contend with. The nearest civilization is far enough away that we don't consider ourselves civilized." She pulled Pamela with her into the yard.

"This is our hideout. No one but us knows the way in and out, and no one leaves here without an escort because my men are trained to shoot first and ask questions later. Do you understand what I'm saying, Miss Charbonneau?"

"I believe so."

"Well just in case there's any question left in your mind, I'm warning you good and hard right now. Don't try to leave or you will die."

"But what of your ransom?" Pamela questioned, almost smugly.

"I don't need a warm body to convince people to pay a ransom note. I can forward them a corpse easier than I can worry about running you down every time you get it in your head to try and escape."

Pamela blanched at the easy way Esther spoke of killing her.

"Now," Esther said, coming to a full stop. "Do you understand me?"

"Yes, I believe I do," Pamela replied, giving the woman her full attention. "My life is obviously in a precarious state of balance, and you are the one who will decide my fate."

Esther smiled. "It's such a pleasure to listen to another intelligent soul speak. I shall enjoy having your company while we decide this matter. Now give me your word that you won't try to leave."

Pamela grimaced. "I promise."

"Good enough."

With that, Esther pulled Pamela toward the rough looking log house. Pamela tried to take in everything. She considered where each building lay in relation to the house, without looking obvious and tried to commit it to memory for later use. The Owens gang would no doubt kill her anyway, so therefore her promise meant nothing. She would seek a means of escape—the sooner the better.

nine

"What do you mean she's gone?" Riley questioned his wife.

A teary-eyed Zandy stood, arms akimbo, shaking her head. "I don't know. I just know that Pamela was with Ruth and me earlier in the evening, but then she took her leave. I thought she'd gone to bed, but when I went up to check on her, she was gone. I've covered the entire house, Riley. She's nowhere to be found."

Riley crossed the room and took Zandy in his arms as she broke into sobs. "Hush, we'll find her. You can't get yourself all worked up. It might harm the babe, and you wouldn't want that."

"But I promised to look out after her," Zandy said in between ragged breaths. "I promised Claudia Charbonneau that no ill would befall her granddaughter. I promised you that I could handle the situation. Now just look. For all I know she could be hurt or even dead!"

"Maybe she's just found a way back to Bradley Rayburn," Riley suggested. At this, Ruth stepped forward and agreed.

"That's right, Zandy. You did say she wanted to get back to him awfully bad. So bad in fact, that the girl's grandmother made you promise not to allow her any money, lest she buy a train ticket home."

"I know," Zandy replied, "but all of her things are still here. Pamela is too devoted to her looks and finery to leave it behind. She would have at least taken as much as she could carry. I checked her room, however. Nothing is missing. Her brushes and combs are still there. And all of her clothes are hanging in the wardrobe, except what she was wearing."

"What was she wearing?" Riley asked. "We'll need to get a description to the sheriff."

"The last I saw," Ruth replied before Zandy could, "she was wearing a white blouse and, I believe, a red skirt."

"Burgundy," Zandy corrected. "It was a burgundy color with black braid trim on the bottom."

Riley led his wife to a brocade chair. "Sit here, and I'll send someone down to the sheriff's office. He'll probably want to look around and see if there's any sign of where she might have gotten off to."

Zandy did as she was instructed. She'd no sooner taken a seat when a fluttering in her abdomen caused her eyes to widen.

"Oh!" she gasped in surprise.

Riley turned sharply to inspect his wife. "What is it? Are you in pain?"

Zandy laughed, amidst her tears, "No, I just felt the baby move!"

Ruth smiled, and Riley seemed stunned. "You felt the baby move?" he questioned. It was still hard to believe that a child actually grew within the yet slender form of his wife.

"I'm sure that was what it was," Zandy answered.

"It's a good sign," Ruth said, coming to pat her stepdaughter's shoulder. "Maybe God has given it to you in order to help you concentrate on something other than Pamela. You need to rest and keep a happy heart for your baby's sake, if not your own."

Riley smiled and knelt down beside Zandy. He took her hand in his and kissed it gently. "You aren't to blame for this. I could never hold you responsible for Pamela's well-being. She's much too headstrong, and we both know it. You have to stay calm for the baby. I'll turn this town upside-down and, no matter how difficult the task, I'll find her. You trust me to do that, don't you?"

Zandy looked deep into the loving eyes of her husband. He gave her great confidence that there was nothing too big for him to undertake. "I do," she whispered.

"Good. Now you and my son need to get to bed. It's late and nothing can be gained by your collapsing on the floor." With that, Riley lifted Zandy into his arms and carried her down the hall.

After seeing his wife to bed, Riley went alone to search the immediate grounds for Pamela. Perhaps she'd fallen asleep somewhere. Riley felt angry that she would be so heartless as to leave Zandy wondering and fretting over her safety. But, even if she had run off, Riley reasoned, he wasn't about to let it bring harm to his wife and child.

Seeing nothing unreasonable, and no sign of a sleeping or otherwise entangled Pamela, Riley decided morning would be soon enough to bother the sheriff. Now, he only had to reason with Zandy and see to it that she kept herself from doing something foolish.

ða

Before Riley could make his way from the house the next morning, a note was delivered by a young boy. Riley looked down at the paper addressed to him and asked the child who'd sent the letter.

"Don't know," the boy said with a shrug. "Somebody I ain't never seen afore. Gave me a nickel and said I should bring this note to you in the mornin'."

Riley opened the folded letter and read:

> *I've taken your wife because you don't deserve
> her. If I'd known of your ways and how you
> planned to force her into a loveless marriage,
> I would never have let you take her. Now she's
> safe and can make the choice for herself.*

Riley reread it quickly, the truth only now starting to stink in. The boy was already halfway down the path, but Riley called him back.

"What did the man look like?" he asked the child, and flipped him another nickel.

The boy's face lit up as he caught the coin. "He weren't any taller than you. He had brown hair. Jes sorta regular lookin'."

"Nothing special about him?" Riley asked. "Think hard."

"Nope," the boy answered, shaking his head. "He was just a man." Riley nodded and let the boy go.

"What's your name, son?" Riley thought to call out.

"Brian," the boy answered. "Brian Masters."

Riley wasted little time. He pushed the note deep into his pocket and went to saddle his horse. It was now all too clear that Pamela had been taken. But, Riley reminded himself with barely controlled rage, it was Alexandra the culprit had been after!

Riley explained the situation to the sheriff and gave all the details of Pamela's disappearance before heading back to the mansion. He left out the news of the note, fearing that if he told anyone, word would get back to Zandy. He had no desire to further worry her with thoughts that someone was after her. Riley wondered what the kidnapper's next step would be, once he realized that Pamela wasn't who he thought she was.

At home, Zandy was already waiting for some word from her husband. She met him at the door and questioned him about his visit with the sheriff.

"Did you tell him that she might have run away?" she asked.

Riley put his arm around her. "No, I think you were probably right. I think someone has taken her."

Burley and Ruth Stewart stood inside the library's open doors. They exchanged a glance before Burley stepped forward. "What makes you so certain, Riley?"

Riley wouldn't give away the fact that he'd received the note, but he had to offer something that seemed logical. "Zandy made a good point as regards Pamela. She wouldn't have left her things behind. Not only that, no money or horses are missing, and the things of value that she owned, like her silver comb and brush, are still on the dresser upstairs."

Burley nodded. "You suppose that Rayburn guy came and took her?"

"I kind of doubt it," Riley said with sigh. Zandy lifted her face to note the weariness in her husband's eyes. She thought she saw fear there too, but dismissed it as Riley continued, "I know Rayburn's type. He's probably already working on another conquest. That's the trouble with young women of means. They often easily fall prey to undesirables who seek only their fortune. Pamela's parents were probably well within their rights to be concerned for their daughter."

Zandy was rather surprised at this proclamation from Riley.

She stared at him a moment, then disengaged herself.

"But what if he wasn't like that? What if they really loved each other, Riley?" she couldn't help but ask.

"Then time and distance won't hurt them, love. Look what happened between us."

Burley interjected, before Zandy could respond, "Besides, that really isn't the issue here. The problem is that Pamela has disappeared, most likely not of her own will. It might be wise if we were to telegraph her parents."

Riley agreed, but added, "I'd like to give it a day or two and see what happens. There's no sense in worrying them if she turns up to have just wandered off in a pout."

"Riley Dawson! Wandered off in a pout?" Zandy was indignant. "What kind of woman do you think Pamela is, anyway? She wouldn't leave us to worry like that."

Riley felt the heat of her words, but didn't dare explain that he wanted to see if the man who'd taken Pamela would return her when he realized she wasn't Zandy. Riley shrugged his shoulders and gave a sheepish grin. "Sorry, I guess I put my foot in that one."

❧

The days that passed waiting for word about Pamela were sheer torture for Zandy and the rest of the household. Riley seemed genuinely worried that Pamela hadn't returned, or at least puzzled that they hadn't received notice giving a clue to her whereabouts.

On the fifth day of Pamela's absence, a letter arrived with the mail. It was from a kidnapper who demanded over one million dollars for Pamela's safe return. Otherwise, the letter stated, she would be killed.

Zandy was present when the letter was received, and Riley, not knowing what the contents were, had no way to shield her from its impact.

"Dear Lord," she whispered in prayer and felt her head grow fuzzy. Never having been one given to fainting, Zandy couldn't even warn her husband before she landed on the floor at his feet.

"Alexandra!" Riley quickly lifted her into his arms. He carried her to a nearby sofa and laid her out. "Ruth!" he shouted into the air. He patted Zandy's face and tried to wake her. He quickly read the note.

"What s wrong, Riley?" Ruth questioned, half running into the room. When she saw Zandy, she emitted a cry of concern and hurried to her side. "What happened?"

"We had a note from Pamela's kidnappers. Zandy read it before I could keep her from it. Next thing I know, she's in a dead faint on the floor," Riley explained.

"Stay here with her," Ruth instructed. "I'll get some smelling salts and a wet cloth." Ruth hurried from the room to retrieve the needed items.

She came back quickly and handed Riley a cloth. "Here," Ruth told Riley, "wipe her face with this." He took it and touched it to his wife's cheek, while Ruth waved the salts under Zandy's nose.

A moan sounded from Zandy as she suddenly came to. She pushed away Ruth's hand and tried to sit up. Riley kept a firm hold on her.

"You just took a nasty fall," he said. "I think you should lie still."

"What happened?" Zandy asked, trying to clear her head.

"You fainted."

Her stepmother's words brought her instantly awake.

"The letter!" she gasped.

"It's all right," Riley assured her. "You have to relax

and let me take care of this."

"But it's all my fault. If I hadn't insisted on bringing her along, she'd be safe back in Missouri with her grandmother. This is all my doing!" She shook her head from side to side, while tears streamed down her cheeks.

Riley took hold of her. "You're always telling me you believe God is in control of our lives. You helped Pamela to God. Don't you realize that she's in His control, and that He watches over His own? I know I've heard you declare the same thing on more than one occasion."

Zandy heard the words, but they offered her no comfort. "Sometimes we grieve God by interfering," she protested. "You said I was sticking my nose in where it didn't belong when we were back home. Maybe this wouldn't have happened if I'd just listened."

"Maybe," Riley admitted. "Then again, maybe it would have happened back there. We can't second-guess this situation. Either you trust God to keep her in His care or you don't. Is God any less God, just because things aren't going your way?"

Zandy realized her husband was right. "No, of course not."

"Good," Riley answered with a smile. "Now, I'm going to carry you upstairs, and I want you to stay in bed for the rest of the day. If you don't, I know ways of putting you to sleep and insuring the matter."

Zandy saw a bit of a twinkle in his eyes and couldn't help but smile. "Very well, Mister Dawson. I shall be an obedient wife."

"That'll be a first," Riley said, lifting her in his arms.

❧

Zandy was true to her word and waited out the day in bed.

In the days that followed the note's arrival, she even tried her best to leave the entire matter in Riley's hands.

She prayed fervently for Pamela's well-being and asked God to send her back safely. She prayed that Riley and the sheriff would have the wisdom to work the matter through and that the entire situation would be resolved quickly.

Mostly she busied herself with Ruth and played with Molly and her brothers. It was almost like old times when she was still at home and a part of their family life.

Riley was grateful for the reprieve from Zandy's usual desire to help. He wanted very much for her to remain calm and at peace, but he knew she was worried for her friend.

Daily, he went to retrieve the mail, always looking for another letter from the kidnappers with further instructions. At one point, he was sitting and considering how he would approach the monetary demands when Burley entered and pulled up a chair.

"Any word yet?" he asked his son-in-law.

"No. I'm getting mighty tired waiting on it, too."

"Kidnappers are queer creatures," Burley said with a shrug. "Who can know their minds?"

"I didn't expect this, though." Riley hadn't intended to speak the words aloud.

"Why not?" Burley questioned. "You were, after all, the one that believed so adamantly that she'd been taken. You were sure of it, in fact, even when it didn't seem all that sensible to me."

Riley said nothing, hoping that Burley would drop the subject. He didn't want to explain the first letter and cause Zandy's father any undue worry. Still, there was the matter of the ransom note. Riley was completely baffled that a man who'd thought Zandy in trouble and wanted to help her out would turn kidnapper when he realized he'd taken the wrong woman. It just didn't figure.

"You're keeping something to yourself, aren't you?" Burley asked seriously. "I think if it involves any of us here, you'd best come clean and share it with me."

Riley ran a weary hand back through his dark hair. There really was no reason that he shouldn't tell Burley. The man had a right to protect his family.

"A boy named Brian Masters brought me a letter the morning after Pamela's disappearance. It explained why she'd been taken. That's how I knew she hadn't just wandered off or run away."

"Why didn't you say so?" Burley questioned. His voice was edged with irritation. "Did you tell the sheriff?"

Riley shook his head and reached into his desk. From the very back of the drawer, he pulled out the letter and handed it to Burley.

Burley unfolded the note and quickly read the contents, then lifted his eyes to meet Riley's. "He meant to take my Zandy?"

"It would appear that way."

"But who would want to do that? I mean, most folks around here know how happy she is. This feller obviously thinks she's being forced to stay with you."

"I've asked myself the same thing, Burley. Who in the world would believe her miserable? She fairly lights up the day with her smile, and the happiness she knows from anticipating this child is more than anyone could doubt. But, what really confuses me is why this same man would now hold Pamela hostage. Why not just return her and lay low for a while? I mean, I realize he would be concerned, since he left the note for me, but he'd have little trouble bringing Pamela back and then disappearing."

"Maybe he read that story you gave the paper," Burley offered.

"I suppose that's a possibility. It was just that I figured if Pamela was seen by other folks, and they knew she was missing, they might offer help in returning her to us," Riley remarked. "I knew her parents were slated to go to the springs in New York, and I didn't figure word would reach them from the article before I had a chance to get word to them myself."

"Maybe this feller realized the potential for a big pay-off. If he knew Pamela was worth a fortune, he might just have decided to make his mistake a profitable one."

Riley shook his head, not knowing what to think. Raising his arms in exasperation, he sighed, "Anything is possible."

Burley handed him back the note and noticed an elaborately scrolled envelope postmarked Washington, D.C. "You in some kind of trouble?" he asked pointing at the letter.

"No," Riley smiled. "In fact, it might be the only truly good thing that's come in the mail in a long while. It seems the honorable Mister Horace Tabor intends to come to Dawson in the near future. It says that he has a matter of great importance to discuss with me."

"Honestly?" Burley seemed dumbfounded. "What could he want?"

"Dawson," Riley replied. "At least I hope that's what he wants."

ten

Pamela lost track of the time. For well over a week, she was confined to a bedroom that was next to the one Esther used for her own. No noise went unchecked, Pamela soon learned, so her attempts to find a way from the house faded into discouragement. The only time she was allowed out of the room was when Esther escorted her to the privy out in back of the house.

Pamela was just as glad to be locked up, however. Each and every time she ventured from the room with Esther, the men would taunt her with lewd comments and whistles. Pamela's cheeks would flame red at some of the things said. Never had she been exposed to such lasciviousness.

Esther laughed at Pamela's innocent embarrassment. It was hard to believe this child could net them such a fortune but, if her sources were right, Esther knew that the Dawsons were already arranging the million dollars.

Pamela tried to pass the time by praying and by thinking of the things Zandy had told her about God. From time to time, her mind lingered on Jim Williams, and then guilt ate at her fiercely.

"He may have taken me from Dawson," Pamela whispered to no one, "but he didn't deserve to die."

She couldn't help but think of Jim's warm brown eyes. A sadness filled her until she forced the image from her mind. "I can't think of this anymore!"

One day, as evening came, Esther appeared with Pamela's

supper. "Venison stew and biscuits," she said and placed the tray on the end of the bed. "Have you still got water in the pitcher?"

"Yes," Pamela said and came forward to peer into the bowl. "I suppose I can't complain that I haven't been well fed. At least, well fed in a rustic kind of fashion."

Esther laughed. "It isn't Delmonico's in New York, that's for sure."

"Delmonico's!" Pamela exclaimed with surprise. "That's one of my parents' favorite places."

"It used to be one of mine, too," Esther admitted. "They served an aspic *de crevette* salad that would bring the world to its feet in applause. I went there every time I could talk someone into taking me."

Pamela shook her head. "And now you're here, kidnapping other socialites? It must seem terribly ironic."

Esther shrugged her shoulders. "It's just the way life is." She turned to leave. "For now," she added, and pulled the door closed.

Pamela sat down to eat and wasn't surprised to find the stew delicious. The biscuits were as light as any she'd ever had, and Pamela hungrily devoured them, knowing that there would be nothing else until morning.

She'd just finished eating when Esther returned, bringing with her a copy of *Peterson's Ladies' National Magazine*. It was patterned after *Godey's Lady's Book* and Pamela knew its issues well.

"I thought you might want to take a look," she said, and tossed the magazine to the bed.

Pamela picked it up and glanced at her captor. "Thank you."

Esther retrieved the dishes. "You'll probably not find

anything terribly useful for your stay with us, but I thought it might break the boredom."

"I wonder if I might make a trip out back before you retire for the evening?" Pamela requested.

"Sure," Esther replied. "I'll take these to the kitchen and be right back." It was a strange, casual sort of relationship between these two women.

Pamela flipped through the magazine while waiting. There was an article on how to arrange cut flowers. Another, equally uninteresting, article gave helpful suggestions for arranging a formal parlor. Of course, there were new dress fashions, and these caught Pamela's eye, but only for a moment. What could she do about them here?

Esther returned and held the door open for Pamela. She obediently walked a pace or two ahead of Esther and wondered if the time would ever come when Esther might drop her guard.

They moved out back through the quarter-moon darkness and passed the place where Esther's sons Joe and Bob were nose to nose in a heated argument.

"Robert Joseph! Joseph Robert! You cut it out here and now. I don't need to break up any childish tantrums tonight. We've got plenty of work that still needs to be done."

The men grudgingly parted company with a "Yessum" muttered under their breath.

Esther continued to the privy with Pamela. "You named them nearly the same thing," Pamela commented.

Esther laughed. "It was their father's doing. He said that way he'd only have the two names to worry about. Don't know what we'd have done if there'd been any more."

"Where's their father now?"

"Dead," Esther said without emotion.

Pamela said nothing more, but cringed as a hideous sound came from where they'd left Esther's sons. Shouts and curses rose on the silent night air and Pamela knew the boys had decided to have a go at one another, after all.

"You see to your business and I'll see to them," Esther said in exasperation. "I swear I'm going to have to beat them both. Grown men ought to know better."

Pamela laughed and did as she was instructed. She could hear the fight raging on and Esther yelling at the top of her lungs. When she stepped away from the outhouse, Pamela was still laughing when suddenly a hand clamped down tight on her mouth. Someone pulled her into the darkness behind the privy.

"This is getting to be a habit," Jim said as he let his hand drop from Pamela's mouth.

"Jim!" Pamela exclaimed, forgetting her predicament. Without realizing what she was doing, Pamela threw her arms around him. "You're alive!"

"Shhh," he said, and embraced her close to him. "You'll get us both killed."

"I thought you were dead already," Pamela said stiffly and pulled away from him. She grew uncomfortable as she realized how much she cared that he was still living.

"Come on," he pulled her away from the buildings and into the darkness. "We have to go!"

Pamela let Jim lead the way without complaint. She feared they would be caught any moment and every sound or missed step was absolute torture. Nevertheless, even when she twisted her ankle, Pamela didn't complain or slow the pace. When Jim began their ascent of the canyon wall, however, Pamela felt moved to speak.

"I can't climb these rocks," she protested. "I know I

haven't the strength."

"You'll do it or stay here," Jim said over his shoulder. "You'd be surprised what a body can do when pushed to do it or die."

Pamela nodded and realized he was probably right. She had no desire to go back and face the wrath of Esther and her gang. "All right," she said with new determination. "Just let me tuck up this skirt, and I'll do it."

"That's the spirit!" Jim whispered. His pride in her choice to fight was evident.

They climbed the canyon wall without once stopping to rest. Jim had picked a place that was lower than the rest of the canyon. He and Caleb had been watching the place for only a couple of days, but it was enough time to learn the routine and make a plan.

They could hear shouting in the yards below and Esther calling for Pamela, but they ignored it and pressed upward. Several times, Pamela felt her strength giving out, but just then, it seemed, Jim would know and reach back to take her hand. His warmth gave her strength and hope.

After what seemed hours, they reached the top, and Pamela was surprised to find another man waiting with two horses.

"Come on over here, little bitty gal," Caleb called in a low voice. "We've got a hard ride ahead of us, and we'd best be about it."

"Who's that?" Pamela questioned, cowering against Jim. He put his arm around her protectively and pulled her forward.

"Caleb Emerson. He's a drifter who saved my life after the Owens gang left me for dead," Jim answered. "Come on," and he lifted her up to the saddle. "We'll have to ride double again."

"No matter," Pamela said gratefully. "If it means getting out of there and back to Dawson, I'd ride an elephant."

"No need for that," Caleb chuckled. "These mounts will do us a whole heap better." With that, they pushed out and rode as fast as they dared. Their horses labored against the altitude, while Pamela shivered as cold mountain winds blew down upon them.

They rode for several hours. Finally, when Pamela knew she couldn't stay another minute atop the horse, Caleb called a halt and began unsaddling his mount.

"We'll camp here tonight," he announced.

"Is it safe? I mean, are we far enough away?" Pamela questioned.

"They'll never find us," Jim said, helping Pamela down. "Caleb and I put out a dozen false trails the night before. Even if they are stupid enough to set out in this darkness, they'll never be able to figure out which way to go first. Once they figure out the real trail, we'll be nearly to Dawson."

Pamela heaved a sigh of relief. "How did you find me?"

"Caleb," Jim said with a nod. "He's drifted these parts for a long time and just happens to be familiar with this gang of thieves."

"Thank you, Mister Emerson." Her long, blond hair whipped around in the wind, giving her an ethereal appearance in the dim light.

"You're welcome, Little Bitty," Caleb said. The nickname surprised her, but Pamela said nothing. "Always glad to help a lady in need," he added with a chuckle, and pointed to where Jim was tethering his horse. "That young man over there nearly fretted himself into the next world worryin' about how to get you back," he whispered against her ear. "So, I'd be sure and thank him proper, too."

Pamela leaned up and gave Caleb's weathered cheek a kiss. The action surprised her almost more than the old man. "I will," she whispered.

Pamela walked back over to where Jim already had a bed fixed for her. "This ought to block out the wind," he said, nodding toward the rocky ledge under which he'd placed her blanket.

"Where will you be?" she asked, straining to see his face. The small amount of moonlight offered little help, and Caleb made no move to put together a fire.

"I'll be right here," Jim assured. "I'm not about to lose you a second time." His words seemed more serious than they needed to be.

Pamela stepped closer. "Thank you for rescuing me, Jim. I know I'm not Zandy, but I appreciate what you've done and risked for me." She leaned up to kiss his cheek as she had with Caleb, but Jim surprised them both by pulling her into his arms. He kissed her full on the lips for just a moment, then released her. The action had taken them both off guard.

Pamela hurried to take her place on the blanket, but before Jim walked away he leaned down to whisper in her ear. "I'm glad you're not Zandy."

Pamela was grateful for the cover of darkness, knowing that she was blushing. Bradley Rayburn's stolen kisses had never left her feeling the way Jim's did. In fact, Bradley was about the farthest thing from her mind at that moment.

She pulled the blanket around her and listened as Jim thanked Caleb for his help.

"It was my pleasure," Caleb told the younger man. "God always gives us a job to do, and often we have to do it alone. But, sometimes He knows we can't stand alone, and then He gives us a friend."

"I'm proud to call you friend, Caleb. I don't know when our paths might cross again, but I'll be there any time you call," he reached out and shook the older man's hand.

"I'm proud to call you friend, too, son," Caleb replied. "You keep your feet firmly planted on God's road and you'll never go wrong. He's a good partner to take on, and you'll never really know what it is to be loved, until you accept His in full."

Pamela felt a strange comforting peace flood her heart. She snuggled down into the blanket and smiled. The contentment she felt was twofold. God had answered her prayers for rescue, and Jim wasn't dead.

eleven

A steady rain was pouring when Pamela awoke the next morning. She was grateful for the small ledge under which Jim had thoughtfully put her bed. Pressing back against the rock wall, Pamela peered out from her blanket and wondered where the men had taken cover.

Suddenly, it seemed too quiet, and Pamela grew fretful. What if the Owens gang had found them and had already done away with Jim and Caleb? Sitting up abruptly, Pamela couldn't help but call out.

"Jim!"

She heard movement to the left and found her fears relieved as Jim scooted under the ledge to sit beside her.

"It looks like it might do this all day," he said with a grin. "I swear, mountain rains are the most unpredictable things."

"Where's Caleb?" Pamela questioned. She could see where Jim's horse was still tethered, but there was no sign of the older man's horse or gear.

"He's gone. Thought it best if we split up, and I figure he's right on that point."

"They'll be coming after us, won't they," Pamela more stated than asked. "A million dollars is nothing to let slip away without a fight. It'll keep them riding the trails, come rain or shine, of that I'm sure."

"A million dollars?" Jim's confusion was evident.

"That's the amount of ransom they asked Riley and Zandy

for," Pamela explained. She pulled the blanket around her to ward off the cold and leaned back against the rock. "They were going to send another letter today and give the details of where they would meet."

Jim's face twisted into a look of disgust. "Why in the world would they think anyone would pay that kind of money?" He realized at Pamela's expression that she was offended by his words. "That didn't come out sounding the way I intended," he immediately added. "It isn't that I wouldn't consider you worth that much money. It's just I can't figure how they would assume Riley Dawson would care enough to part with that much."

Pamela calmed her singed emotions. The last person in the world she wanted to fight with was Jim. "The leader of the gang is a woman. She's very intelligent and has her people bring her newspapers from Denver. Apparently, when you took me from Dawson, Riley and Zandy must have put out a story with my picture, in hopes that someone would know something about my disappearance. The only thing is, the story told too much of my background and the fact that I'm from a wealthy family in Kansas City."

"Are your folks that rich?" Jim questioned innocently. He turned his face to stare deep into Pamela's blue eyes. Her face held a gentle expression, almost one of endearment. Jim couldn't help but realize how short the distance between his face and hers was.

"My folks are very well off," Pamela whispered. "I'm their only child and I stand to inherit a great deal. That's why they didn't trust Bradley Rayburn."

At the spoken name of the man she loved, Jim's fascination with Pamela's delicate face ended abruptly. He tried to distance himself by moving away just a bit, but Pamela would have no part of it.

"It's so cold. I know it isn't proper, and it would be most unacceptable were the circumstances different, but I wonder if you would mind...I mean," she paused as Jim looked back at her. "Would you sit very close and maybe even put your arm around me?"

Her eyes were so innocent in their pleading glance that Jim swallowed hard and moved closer. Taking the blanket, he pulled it around both of their shoulders and let Pamela move under his arm to lean against his chest. He could feel her trembling and wondered if it was only the cold or if he affected her the same way she did him.

Pamela tried to seem oblivious to the physical contact while, in truth, she was shocked with herself for suggesting such a thing. After a few moments of silence, she spoke of a matter on which she'd reflected for most of the night.

"I heard some of what Caleb said to you last night," she began. "His words about God were so comforting, and I truly felt that I was protected under God's care. I was just wondering, are you a Christian, too?"

Jim sighed, releasing a bit of the tension he felt. Holding Pamela in his arms was almost painful in light of the memory that she loved someone else. It shouldn't matter, Jim reminded himself. He still had to figure out what to do about Zandy.

"I guess so," he said in a noncommittal way. "I asked to be saved when I was just a boy, but I've never really done anything that would prove that it took. Caleb told me to seek God out and ask His forgiveness. He said a lot of times we're inclined to get sidetracked. God knows we aren't strong creatures, and that's why He's so good about forgiving us. I guess right now I'm just trying to work things out so that I can be on good terms with Him again."

Pamela smiled. "I went to church with nannies and maids. Sometimes, once in a very long while, I would go with my parents. But you know, until I met Zandy, I hadn't a clue what God was truly about. How can somebody sit in church, listen to the preacher tell of hell fire and eternal damnation, and still not understand that they needed saving?"

"I don't guess I have the answer to that one either," Jim replied. "I never was one for church after Ma died. For that matter, I've never been one for much of anything."

"What do you want to do with your life, Jim?" Pamela asked softly.

"I can't rightly say," Jim responded. "I've tried my hand at mining, cattle, horses, farming, and I was even a lawman for Riley Dawson when he first came to Colorado."

"Back when he was so very evil?"

"Yeah," Jim replied. "But I suppose he's changed now, eh?"

Pamela lifted up her head and met Jim's dark brown eyes. "He honestly has, Jim. Zandy is very happy with him now."

"I guess I'm glad for that," Jim said, and grew thoughtful. "If Riley can change that much, I guess God won't have such a hard time with me."

Pamela laughed out and the sound echoed off the rock ledge overhead. "That's the same kind of thing I told Zandy when she helped me to find God's direction for my life. I figured if one man could be so changed from the worst possible character to the kind of person I saw in front of me, then I knew God could help me. I guess I'd come to the place where I had nothing and no one else."

"What about your Mister Rayburn?"

Pamela shrugged. It was funny how over the last week or so, she'd given much more thought to Jim than Bradley. "I'm not sure. I suppose my parents could have been right. They could also have been wrong. I think when we go back to Missouri, I'll sit down and write a long letter and apologize for the way I treated them. I suppose we'll just have to work it out from there."

"You've changed," Jim said suddenly. He didn't wish to break the fragile peace between them, but Pamela had obviously matured a great deal in the days of her capture.

"I suppose I have," Pamela replied, not taking the slightest bit of offense. "I had so much time to think about things. I realized how demanding I was and how bitter and angry I'd grown. Being in a place where the only thing people thought of was how much money they could make off you, I realized how much I'd harmed the ones I loved."

"How so?" Jim questioned.

"At the Owenses', nobody cared if I wanted things done a certain way. No one gave a thought to how I dressed or what I ate. I was totally and completely at their mercy and that caused me to see how demanding I've always been. The rest...well, I think a lot of my reason for wanting to marry Bradley had to do with making my parents take notice of me." The words surprised Pamela, for she'd never truly allowed the revelation to surface in full. Speaking them seemed to validate the possibility, however, and she felt relieved for having said them.

"I did...do...love Bradley," she continued. "But I'm not sure that I understand in full what that even means. Zandy told me about God's love and how He loved us enough to send Jesus, His only son, to die for me and all the other people in the world. And all because if He didn't, we could never get close to God. God's love for me is such a wonder that I can't begin to imagine."

Jim felt his eyes lock with Pamela's. "I know what you mean," he said hoarsely. The words would barely make themselves heard. "Caleb made me realize the same thing. I'm glad God cares enough to not have given up on me. I feel in many ways like I've just been saved. Maybe that's the truth of the matter. Either way, I'm just a babe at this walking with God stuff."

Pamela sat up with a smile. "Yes, that's it exactly. I'm so much an infant when it comes to understanding God and the Bible. I've never even given much of a reading to the Word of God, yet Zandy says it holds all the answers for our lives."

Jim smiled. "Zandy would say that. I remember her faith well. I always admired her for it and wondered how a person could give themselves over so completely to something like a book filled with words. Now, though, I think I'm beginning to understand."

Pamela leaned back against Jim and nodded her head in agreement. "It's like God calling the heart to a new way of beating."

"I guess we have that in common, anyway," Jim said, not thinking.

"What do you mean?"

"Being new Christians," he replied. "We're both just starting a new way of living, and both of us have a heap to learn."

❧

It was nearly two hours later before the rain let up. Jim knew the flooding in the valley below would most likely be bad. He took Caleb's suggestion of heading down an obscure little path that led into Central City, offering a silent prayer that God would give them safe passage.

Easing into the saddle behind Pamela, Jim was more than a little aware of her close presence. It was becoming increasingly difficult for Jim to ignore the fact that he had, indeed, come to care about this "little bitty gal."

twelve

A great cloud of disorder and lawlessness settled over Dawson. That, along with the heavy rains, left decent folk confined to their homes. Riley watched the situation with growing apprehension. When the town wasn't busy burying those who'd been shot or knifed in the streets, it was building gallows for those who'd committed the crimes.

Riley insisted that Zandy, Ruth, and the children remain inside the mansion. He hired extra men to police the grounds and watched every shadow with a wary eye. The problem continued to grow by leaps and bounds, and there seemed to be nothing Riley could do to change the immediate circumstances.

One idea continued to give him hope of at least taking his loved ones from the conflict. Horace Tabor had made him a very substantial buy-out offer. Riley hated to just walk away from the town. The fact was, he felt largely responsible for what it had become. He was the one who'd brought the town back to life when it was nothing more than a ghost town called Temperance. He was the one who'd taken possession of the mines through gambling and underhanded dealings. Was God now making him face the fruit of his past labors?

Shaking his head, Riley pulled out the Bible. He longed to spend more and more time reading the pages of this book. He forever felt inadequate when it came to being the spiritual leader of his family. Zandy knew much more, in the sense of having years of Bible stories and reading in her memory. The times when he tried to guide or direct them in some choice or decision, Zandy inevitably upstaged him with some Scripture that left him feeling stupidly misguided.

His salvation was real, of that he was certain. His spirit was in close communion with God. That, too, was undeniable. Why, then, couldn't he be the husband Zandy needed? What was it that kept him from being a proper spiritual leader in his home?

A knock on the door brought his attention from the open Bible.

"Come in," he called, pushing back from the desk. The large leather chair creaked in protest as Riley got to his feet.

Zandy entered the room. Her face was radiant, even though a frown lined her lips. Her worry for Pamela was evident, as was her growing condition. Riley watched her cross the room to him. He couldn't help but smile, and he placed a hand against the delicately belted blouse that covered the oversized waist of her skirt.

"And how are my two most favorite people today?" he asked softly.

Zandy's eyes met his, and Riley couldn't keep from moving his hands to cup her face. "We're fine," she answered with the hint of a smile. "Have you had any word?"

Riley shook his head. "I imagine we'll hear soon enough. And when we do, I'll be ready. In the meantime, I think I've made a decision about Mister Tabor's offer."

"Oh?" her eyes widened in anticipation of what her husband would say.

"Yes," Riley replied and rubbed his thumb against her cheek. "I believe I will sell all of my holdings in Dawson to him."

"Truly, Riley?" Zandy reached up to take hold of his hands. "Can we honestly be rid of this awful place?"

"The offer Tabor made is generous, and I can't help but believe there comes a time when a man has to walk away from his mistakes and start anew. Tabor believes he can control this riffraff with his own style of law and order. He has far more power and say than I could ever hope to hold, or even want to, for that matter. When I told him about the difficulties we'd been having with the Owens gang and other like them, Horace Tabor actually laughed."

"Laughed?" Zandy asked.

"Yes," Riley admitted. He kissed his wife's hands and pulled her with him to the sofa. They sat side by side, with Riley's arm protectively around Zandy. She hesitated only a moment before leaning her head against Riley's muscular shoulder.

"Is it that Mister Tabor is confident he can control the evil element in this town, or is he so much a part of their world that it no longer bothers him?" Zandy finally questioned.

"I don't honestly know," Riley replied. "Whatever his thoughts on the matter, I'll simply be glad to be rid of this place."

"Me too," Zandy wholeheartedly agreed. Suddenly, it dawned on her that her father and stepmother would be without a job and home. "What about my family?" she asked.

"I've already considered their needs. I'll give your

father enough money to start over wherever he'd like. I think he'll be relieved to get the children out of Dawson," Riley answered.

"I know Ruth will be," Zandy said, remembering something her stepmother had said earlier. "She told me the boys had picked up bad language at school. I guess the schoolmaster has no control over the larger boys, and the younger ones seem to just naturally fall into bad habits."

"Well," Riley began, the frustration in his voice evident, "I'm grateful for now that the school term is finished. By the time fall rolls around, we'll be long gone, if I have anything to say about it."

Zandy felt the baby give a sharp kick. "I think that suits your son as well."

Riley smiled at her reference to a boy. "Coming around to my way of thinking, eh, Mrs. Dawson?"

Zandy smiled, "Occasionally, it seems to agree with me to do so."

Riley returned her smile and placed a kiss on her temple. "First things first, however. We'll do all we can to get Pamela back. Did I tell you that her parents wired me to say that someone will be arriving in Dawson to see to their interest in this matter? Imagine, your only child is taken hostage, and you do nothing more than arrange to send someone on your behalf."

Zandy shook her head. "I told you that Pamela had a bad home life."

"Yes, I know. But, I told you that we can't save her from all the hurts and pains that this world will offer. Only God can do that. Remember?"

Zandy nodded with a sigh. "But it is so hard to do nothing."

"Like you once told me, often we have to live through the rough times in order to learn from the choices we've made in error. Either way, God is still God, and He's the one dealing the hand, so to speak. And, Jesus is right there too, always coming to His father on our behalf. In fact, I was just reading an interesting verse," Riley stated, and went to retrieve the Bible from his desk. "It says here in Hebrews seven, verse twenty-five, 'Wherefore he is able also to save them to the uttermost that come unto God by him, seeing he ever liveth to make intercession for them.' That verse is about Christ and the fact that He always lives to intervene for you and me. Imagine that Alexandra," he said, using her given name.

Zandy couldn't help but warm under his excitement. "I've honestly not ever read that Scripture before. It's wonderful, and I'm glad you shared it with me."

Riley felt strengthened in his role of leader by her statement. "If Jesus is interceding for us, and the Holy Spirit is interceding for us, as Romans eight, twenty-six says, how can we possibly doubt that God will hear our petitions?"

Zandy was truly in awe of her husband's astute insight. God was helping her to see that Riley was more than worthy of her trust and admiration.

Before she could speak, the housekeeper came to announce that Pamela's uncle had arrived. Riley and Zandy went quickly to greet him.

"I'm Riley Dawson and this is my wife, Zandy," he said, stepping forward to take the stranger's hand.

"Robert Charbonneau," the man replied. He was nearly matched in height to Riley's tall frame and had pale blue eyes that seemed somehow harsh. "Have you had further word on my niece's whereabouts?"

"No, but I expect to hear almost any time," Riley stated.

"I had the carriage driver bring me here first, just in case she'd already been returned," Robert said. "I'll take a room at the hotel."

"Nonsense," Riley interrupted. "We've over twelve unoccupied bedrooms in this house. There is surely no need for you to stay in town. Besides, the kidnapper knows to contact us here. You'll want to stay close in order to keep informed the very minute we get notification."

Robert nodded. "I appreciate that Mister Dawson."

"Please call me Riley. I'll have someone bring in your luggage. Would you care for something to eat or drink, Mister Charbonneau?"

"That would be very much to my liking," Robert admitted, "but you must call me Robert if I am to call you Riley."

"Deal," Riley said with a smile.

"Come along, gentlemen," Zandy said, leading the way. "I'll have Cook provide us with some sandwiches and lemonade."

༺ঙ

That afternoon, the second ransom letter arrived and with it the instructions for the exchange of money. Robert Charbonneau was unemotional as he read, then reread the letter, while Riley waited in silence.

"Do you have any idea who's holding her?" Robert asked, handing the letter back to Riley.

"I thought at first that I did," Riley replied. "The reason being, and this is in strictest confidence, the kidnapper originally intended to take my wife."

"Your wife?" Robert's surprise seemed to justify further explanation.

"A long time ago, there was a man who was interested in

my wife. He left town thinking that she was being forced into a loveless marriage with me," Riley explained. He'd only come to remember Jim Williams' interest in Zandy over the last week or so. "I don't know for sure that it was the same man who took Pamela, but he did leave a note explaining that his intention had been to rescue Zandy from me."

"I see," Robert said rather stiffly. "So Pamela's life has been endangered because some lovesick idiot thought to make some grandiose gesture toward your wife?"

"I suppose you could put it that way. However," Riley stated, meeting the man eye to eye, "I question whether it's still the same man who's sending the ransom notes."

"Why do you say that?"

"I ran a story in the Denver paper. It might have been foolhardy and brought us undesired attention in the matter of Pamela's disappearance. In fact, it is entirely possible that the person responsible for the ransom demands is just someone who learned of Pamela's disappearance and hoped to make a tidy profit."

"I suppose that is a possibility," Robert had to admit. "But why would the man who hoped to rescue your wife still have my niece?"

"That's what I don't understand," Riley replied. "Unless of course, she talked him into helping her get back to Kansas City and that Bradley Rayburn character."

"I'll wire back to the house so they can be on the lookout, but Rayburn isn't even in Kansas City anymore."

"Where is he?" Riley couldn't help but ask.

"On his honeymoon," Robert answered dryly. "It seems in his pining for my niece, he up and married the first wealthy widow who'd have him. They're now in Europe, or so the papers all say."

Riley shook his head. "Let's hope she didn't go back home, then."

&

After Robert Charbonneau had telegraphed the Charbonneau residence, he stepped into the muddy streets of Dawson. The rain had temporarily stopped.

Robert intended to see to the matter of Pamela's safe return. Having enjoyed life as a man of means, Robert thought he knew that money was often the only way to accomplish anything. Going into the first saloon he passed, he quickly sized up the clientele and began the task of rounding up men-for-hire who would go out in pursuit of his niece and those who held her captive.

"You understand," Robert said to the seedy crowd. "I will pay you each ten dollars now and another twenty when you return with her. But, you must see to it that the kidnapper is brought in alive. I want to watch his neck stretched from the gallows when they declare him guilty."

The men around him nodded their approval and held out their hands for the pay. Robert did as he promised and sent them on their way in search of Pamela. Riley Dawson might take comfort in waiting the abductors out, but he didn't. He was a man used to taking matters into his own hands and this time would be no exception!

thirteen

Making her way through the muddy streets of Central City, Colorado, Pamela realized that she'd begun to savor Jim's quick sense of humor and open honesty. Enjoying the companionship of a man such as Jim had never been in Pamela's agenda. He was ill educated, dirt poor, and socially deficient. Beyond that he needed a shave, haircut, and thorough washing. Under normal circumstances, Pamela would have considered him totally worthless. But there was something more to Jim than met the eye. Something that Pamela could no longer ignore.

She couldn't help but smile, watching him lead the horse through the town. He tried hard to avoid the messier places in the road, but all of it seemed to hopelessly ooze muck.

Central City was much the same as Dawson. It was yet another of the infamous mining communities that had seemingly sprung to life overnight. Saloons and gambling houses lined the path while dry goods stores, apothecaries, and other businesses were interlaced between them. Jim finally settled on the nearest store of respectable appearance and tethered the horse to the hitching post.

"I'll see what I can do about getting us some grub. I don't have much left in the way of money, but maybe I can trade for something." Giving a look up and down the street, Jim lifted Pamela from the horse and carried her to the boardwalk. "I think you'd best stay close to me," he whispered in her ear.

Pamela readily agreed, finding the raucous laughter and swaggering patrons of the nearest bar a bit unnerving. She was only too aware of the sheltered life she'd lived. Although she and Bradley had spent many of their evenings on the town, the upper crust of Kansas City had never associated with the likes of what she was exposed to at the present. But her feelings weren't a matter of snobbery here. They were a matter of survival.

Latching onto Jim's arm in a possessive manner, she missed the smile that crossed his face for a brief, fleeting moment. He liked the way she needed him just then. It made him feel good to know that she had come to trust what he represented versus what these drunken strangers personified. Tucking her arm tight against him, Jim made his way into the store.

Several miners milled about the narrow room. Some seemed intent on tools at hand, others just drifted around aimlessly. Pamela squeezed closer to Jim and when she did, she accidentally stepped on his foot.

"Oh!" she exclaimed, startled and in complete embarrassment. "I'm so sorry."

Jim chuckled. "No problem. I only walk on the bottoms." Pamela tried to smile, but in truth she was scared to death. When several gunshots sounded outside, she felt herself grow faint. Life in the past few weeks had offered her more excitement than she desired.

"Can I help you?" the shopkeeper asked from behind a filthy counter.

Jim began to talk with the man, while Pamela tried not to notice the noise outside. She was lost in thought until her eye spied a Denver newspaper. Completely forgetting her fear, Pamela stepped away from Jim and took a copy of the paper from the counter. She scanned the front page, wondering if anything else had been written about her disappearance. Seeing nothing there, she continued to flip through the pages until her eye caught a startling announcement. Pamela's hands began to shake as she reread the tiny article.

> *Mrs. Alison Timbre of Kansas City married Mister Bradley Rayburn in an elaborate ceremony on Saturday. Mrs. Timbre, formerly Alison Cavanaugh of the Chicago Cavanaughs, is said to be worth several million dollars and intends to finance her husband's new business, which is yet to be announced. The couple will set up housekeeping after touring Europe for the summer.*

There was a dry ache in her throat and for some reason, Pamela couldn't seem to put the paper down. How could Bradley have married this woman? *He said he loved me. He promised he'd wait forever to be at my side again,* Pamela thought to herself. Now only months after her father's ugly scene at their engagement party, Bradley was touring Europe with his new wife.

She didn't realize when Jim had come to stand behind her. She glanced up when she felt his hand brush hers at the paper's edge. Their eyes met. The pain was so evident in hers, while the sympathy in his was spoken in a mere look. He took the paper from her, replaced it on the counter, then led her out of the store and back to the horse.

Her vision blurred and Pamela was grateful that Jim held her arm firmly against his waist. She never thought to ask him how he'd fared in getting provisions. All she could think of was the fact that Bradley had found someone else. A very rich someone else.

"I'm sorry Pamela," Jim said, lifting her into the saddle. He stuffed their supplies into the saddlebags and came up behind her, somehow believing he could offer her more comfort if he stayed close at hand.

They rode from the town in silence, while all around them was utter chaos. Pamela didn't even notice. She felt the numbing of her shock as it seemed to spread through her veins, leaving her cold and dead.

How could he? I loved him, she thought. *I gave my heart to him and refused to hear any ill of him whatsoever. I stood up for him before my father and mother and argued with all that I could dream up to convince them that he was more than the ne'er-do-well that they saw. Now, they've proven their insight to be correct and I'm the fool.*

In complete defeat, she slumped back against Jim. The tears gave way and poured from her eyes. There was nothing left to go home to. No reason to go on.

Jim tightened his hold on the reins and in doing so, tightened his hold on Pamela. She appeared so frail and broken, and his heart ached to make everything better. He struggled for something to say, some encouragement he could whisper into her ear, but nothing came to mind. She was just a little bitty gal, he reasoned, just like Caleb had nicknamed her. How could she possibly be called upon to bear up under such devastating news?

Jim felt like kicking himself for having allowed his feelings for Pamela to deepen. What he'd convinced himself was just admiration and friendship felt like considerably more in the wake of seeing her obvious attachment to a man who'd jilted her so completely.

He could feel the sobs racking her body, and it nearly deprived him of his self-control to seem unmoved. He kept reminding himself that what she didn't need was another man romancing her with sweet words and eloquence. Not that he had either.

He was doing fine at hiding his feelings until Pamela lowered her face into her hands. It was as if she thought she could somehow block out the world and all that hurt her.

"Hush," he whispered against her hair. "Shhh. Crying won't help." The words seemed to settle her a bit, and Jim tried to think of something more to say. Finally it came to him in a startling revelation. "God's with you Pamela. He won't let you bear this alone."

Pamela lifted her face and turned to meet Jim's eyes. She nodded, knowing that Jim spoke the truth. What she didn't expect were the words that he added upon seeing her tear-streaked face.

"I won't let you bear it alone, either." The words were simple, yet they spoke volumes to Pamela's weary heart and mind. Somehow, just hearing them made the situation more tolerable.

Pamela managed to put her tears aside and, when Jim felt she was better composed, he began to converse on anything and everything to keep her mind from her misery.

She heard him say something about being in Dawson by morning, but it didn't register as being important. In her mind, Pamela was replaying the events of her life. She thought of first meeting Bradley and how she'd fallen helplessly in love with his gallant nature and zest for life.

Considering these matters, Pamela realized that what hurt the most was the fact that her parents had been absolutely right about Bradley. He was hunting a fortune, and with Pamela he'd found one. She was wealthy and fully capable of seeing to his needs, which, as Pamela couldn't help but remember, included starting a new business venture with several of his close friends. He would never really divulge what type of business he intended to found, but then again, Pamela had never cared. She'd openly promised that whatever it took, she'd make Bradley's dreams come true, just as he had made hers a reality.

But now there was nothing left of that dream. She chided herself mentally for being so gullible. She seethed in rage, considering all the things he'd said to her. The promises he'd made. The future he'd planned. All of it was to be theirs together, and now he was living those dreams with another woman. His wife!

By the time the sun started fading behind the mountain peaks, Pamela was no longer hurt. She was mad. Enraged at her stupidity and appalled at the fool Bradley Rayburn had made of her, Pamela became sullen and stiff. She no longer leaned against Jim for support and the change in her was evident to him.

He wanted to say something, but what could he say that he hadn't already said? He couldn't very well tell her that he was starting to have feelings for her. He couldn't say anything without jeopardizing the thin veneer of friendship that had developed between them. He was still the man who'd taken her from Dawson, Jim reminded himself. He had been solely responsible for her plight from the moment he'd taken her from Zandy and Riley's care. How could he offer her anything that would matter?

Without warning, Jim reined back on the horse and dismounted. It had suddenly become unbearable to be that near her. Just thinking the thoughts he had contemplated made Jim painfully aware that he'd come to care a great deal more for Pamela Charbonneau than he'd ever thought possible.

If Pamela thought his actions strange, she said nothing. Her face was frozen in a disinterested stare that was fixed straight ahead. Jim doubted she saw anything but the images in her mind.

Leading the horse forward, he could only offer up a prayer for God's intervention. Jim found himself begging God to ease her pain and set things right again. He could only silently wish that things might have been different between them. With a shake of his head, Jim began the descent toward the roadway that would take them back to Dawson. It had once been home, he reminded himself. Now it was just a place of reckoning, and Jim couldn't help but wonder what fate awaited him there.

fourteen

Pamela couldn't sleep that night. She restlessly paced the ground just outside the campfire's circle of light. She had no desire for Jim to see the anguish in her face. She was so confused and angry. Why did her heart have to be so willing to jump in where others had bade her to see reason? Why, oh why, did they all have to be so right about Bradley Rayburn?

In complete frustration, Pamela finally plopped down on the ground where Jim had left her a blanket. The summer air was surprisingly cold, and Pamela suddenly realized that she'd taken a chill. Shivering down under the cover, Pamela stared blankly into the fire and was almost startled to find Jim's eyes staring back from across the way. She had thought him asleep.

Without smiling or nodding, she acknowledged his gaze with a look, then closed her eyes, hoping against hope to blot out the events of the day and the raging emotions that surged through her heart.

Pamela awoke with a start to find it was still dark. She sat up and, noticing that the fire was getting low, retrieved a few pieces of wood and stirred up the flames. Sitting back down, Pamela hugged her knees to her chest and rested her chin. The fire crackled and popped, while the yellow flames danced in a hypnotic frenzy. She watched the performance for some time, wondering why she couldn't find peace for the situation at hand.

"God," she prayed in a whisper, "I don't know what to do. I feel so hurt, so betrayed. Yet, it isn't really that at all. I feel like a fool." She nodded silently to the fire. Yes, that was what bothered her the most. Pamela Charbonneau was used to having her own way. She'd rarely been challenged and now, she felt ridiculous and stupid in the wake of Bradley's marriage to someone else.

"My parents were right, as were the others who tried to warn me. How stupid I am, Lord," Pamela sighed. It was then that she realized that she didn't even love Bradley. "I don't love him," Pamela declared to the fire. "How could I have been so convinced that I did?"

The wind moaned down through the trees and whispered softly against the silent night. The fire died down to a gentle, quiet glow and with it, Pamela decided to try again to sleep.

"I've been so blind, God," she whispered to the starry sky overhead. "Feelings I thought I had were nothing more than the rebellious imaginations of a spoiled child. I just wanted to get back at my parents for never being there. For never loving me." The realization that this was her heart's most deeply buried secret produced the same effect as if a weight were lifted from her shoulders.

"I still don't know what to do or how to make amends. Oh, God, help me to see clearly what Your Will is for my life. Help me to recognize the heart's calling, when the real love of my life comes along." Aching and lonely, Pamela pulled the covers tightly around her shoulders and fell into a troubled sleep. She had no way of knowing that across the fire, Jim Williams had listened in feigned sleep to her prayers and wondered if somewhere in her pain-filled heart, there might be room for him.

a

The road into Dawson was barely dry enough for   passage and Jim took special care to lead the horse, while Pamela nervously fidgeted with the saddle horn.

"I'm sorry I was such poor company yesterday," Pamela called down to Jim. "I had a hard time dealing with the shock of what Bradley did, but I'm much better now."

Jim glanced up and smiled. "I'm glad to hear that. I knew God would see you through."

Pamela returned the smile with one of her own. "I intend to tell everyone how you rescued me from the Owens gang. I even hope to encourage my parents to give you a reward."

"No," Jim replied, shaking his head. "That would be totally uncalled for. If it weren't for me, you'd never have been taken from the safety of the Dawson house. I have a lot to own up to, and one of the first things I got to do is face up to Riley Dawson for what I planned to do in the first place."

"He doesn't have to know," Pamela insisted.

"He already does," Jim answered. "I left him a note, and even though I didn't sign it, I'm sure he knows it was me."

Pamela didn't say anything. She didn't know what she could say. Jim had his own problems to resolve, just as she had hers. She knew she still needed to sort through things with her parents and, for that matter, to confess her misdirection and rebellion to Riley and Zandy. After all, she reasoned, she'd put them through plenty of complaining and bitterness. They had a right to see her humbled and sorry.

They were just rounding the final bend, when they were suddenly surrounded by six riders. All the men were heavily armed and pulled their guns to halt Jim and Pamela's progress.

"Dear Lord," Pamela whispered prayerfully, feeling her heart catch in her throat. Her first thought was that these men were somehow connected to Esther Owens and her gang of thugs.

"What do you want?" Jim questioned the men. "We ain't got much to hand over, so if it's cash or goods you're looking for, you're out of luck."

"We ain't after loot," a particularly seedy character replied. He pushed his horse forward just a bit until it stood nose to nose with the one Pamela rode.

"What's your name?" the man asked Pamela. His cold hard stare caused her to tremble.

"Pa...Pa," she stuttered, "Pamela. Pamela Charbonneau."

"That's what we figured. Your uncle hired us to find you and bring you back. This here man is going to be under arrest for kidnappin' you."

"He didn't kidnap me!" Pamela exclaimed. "Well, not intentionally. He did, however, rescue me from outlaws who intended to hold me for ransom."

"I don't see as it's any of my business," the man replied. "The boys and me were hired to bring you back. We get a hefty balance when that's done, and I don't much care how the matter gets solved with this here man after that. You're coming with me, and he's going to jail. You and your uncle can work out the details later."

"Now, wait just a minute," Jim protested.

"No, you wait a minute," the seedy man spoke. He reached down and yanked the reins from Jim's hands. "We got you out-numbered and out-gunned. I don't want to kill you, but if you won't come right quietly, I'll do what I got to do."

"No!" Pamela cried. "He's innocent!"

"I don't much care, ma'am," the man replied. "I'm getting paid to do a job. It's the first job I've had myself in weeks so I intend to do what I'm told and collect my money."

Pamela cast a pleading glance at Jim. He seemed surprisingly calm, almost relieved.

"Jim, I promise I'll get my uncle to see reason. He doesn't understand what's happened. I don't even know how or why he's here, but I'll straighten everything out," she said. She watched as Jim was moved away from the horse and surrounded by four of the men.

"We'll be takin' you on back to your kin, now," the man said to Pamela. Leading her horse down the road, Pamela glanced back with a look of helplessness on her face. "I'll send someone to the jail, Jim. I promise." Jim's dark eyes met hers across the distance and left Pamela with a strange feeling. Why did she suddenly care so much what happened to him?

&

By the time they reached the Dawson mansion, Pamela was nearly hysterical. She had to find a way to make everyone understand that Jim was sorry for his involvement in her disappearance.

When they came to a halt just to the side of the house, Pamela threw herself off the horse and, hiking up her skirt in a most unladylike fashion, she made a dash for the front of the house.

"Uncle Bob!" she yelled, pushing back the huge door. "Uncle Bob!"

The room was instantly filled with people. Zandy came from one direction with Riley right behind her, while Robert Charbonneau appeared from the opposite direction where he'd been working in the library. Burley and then Ruth, with Molly on her hip, came from upstairs, and Zandy's little brothers moved in behind Pamela through the open door.

"Pamela!" Robert said, instantly taking his niece into his arms. "You're alive and safe. Did he hurt you?"

"Uncle Bob, you must help me!" Pamela pleaded, pushing away from his embrace.

"I will, Sugar. I will. Just tell me everything and I'll see to it that your abductor gets his just rewards," Robert replied. He reached out to push back his niece's disheveled hair, but she would have no part of it.

"You don't understand," she said, nearly in tears. She was exhausted beyond her means, having slept so very little the night before. "I have to talk to you about this. You can't put him in jail."

Robert shook his head in confusion. "Put who in jail?"

"Jim," Pamela replied. "You have to let him go. He saved me from the Owens gang. He risked his life. He didn't mean to take me. Your men have taken him to jail and he's not responsible."

"Your men?" Riley questioned with a sharp glance at Robert Charbonneau.

"Pammy, you're making no sense," Robert said, trying to soothe her. He had no desire to get into an argument with Riley over the hiring of some local thugs.

Zandy stepped forward and put her arms around Pamela. "You're exhausted. Come have a bath and some rest. Are you hungry?"

Pamela shook her head. She didn't know whether or not she was hungry. All she knew was that Jim was going to jail for nothing more than a terrible misunderstanding.

"You have to listen to me," Pamela said, sobbing the words. "You have to listen!"

Robert stood back, uncertain what to do. Riley looked on just as helplessly, as did Ruth and Burley. Zandy looked up at Robert and, with a nod, turned Pamela toward the stairs.

"Robert, I'm taking Pamela to have a hot bath. Please see to her concerns about this, ah, Jim?" she said with a questioning look at Pamela.

"That's right. Jim," she said, clinging tightly to Zandy's arm. "Jim Williams. You know him, Zandy. He said you did."

Zandy couldn't have been more stunned. Jim Williams had not crossed her mind in a very long time. The last time she'd seen him had been before she'd married Riley. He'd accused her of spending the night with Riley and with his announcement that he was leaving Dawson, Colorado, left Zandy without a single friend in the world.

After staring at Pamela with her mouth open in surprise, Zandy lifted her gaze to meet Riley's eyes. Amazingly enough, he didn't seem at all surprised.

"Are you all right, Zandy?" he questioned.

Zandy nodded. "You'd better see to Jim, and I'll take care of Pamela."

"Let me help you," Ruth said, putting Molly down to run her own way. "Burley, you'd best keep an eye on her, or she'll be tearing down the draperies again."

Burley nodded and went in the direction of his youngest child, while Ruth moved to Pamela's side. "I'll have the bath readied," she said, and went ahead of Zandy and Pamela on the stairs.

Pamela refused to move until she'd stressed her concerns once again to Robert. "Please, Uncle Bob, don't let them hurt Jim. He's not the one you want."

Robert started to speak, but Zandy wisely shook her head. "I'm sure your uncle will do what is necessary to see to justice. Right now, Pamela, you must rest."

Pamela finally gave in to Zandy's mothering and allowed her to lead her from the room. Riley and Robert faced off in the open vestibule, each wondering what the other would say first.

"You hired men to go after her?" Riley questioned.

Robert shrugged. "I had to do what I could to ensure she came home safely. Your sheriff and his men didn't seem capable of doing the job, so I offered an incentive to men who could."

"You could have jeopardized everything and gotten her killed. Besides that, what if she's telling the truth? What if Williams isn't responsible for the ransom notes?"

"It doesn't matter," Robert replied. "She's back, and at this point I only want to know what Williams has done to her, and then I intend to see him hanged from the nearest tree! Right now, however, I have some business to settle." With that, Robert stormed off, leaving Riley to stare after him.

fifteen

Pamela had to admit she felt better after the bath, but she refused to sleep until Zandy agreed to sit at her side and listen to every word of her ordeal.

"I just have to make someone understand," she said in a way that Zandy couldn't ignore.

With a nod, Zandy moved to the bed and took a seat beside her friend. "Then tell me everything."

"You do remember Jim Williams, don't you?" Pamela asked.

"Of course, I do. Jim and I were once good friends. I thought he cared a great deal about me, but it turned out—"

"He did care. Does still, for that matter. He planned to take you that night, instead of me," Pamela interrupted.

"What?"

"He only knew about the person Riley used to be, and apparently someone told him, long after you had come to love Riley, that you'd been forced into marriage. Jim thought he was responsible because of the way he had treated you. He told me that he hated himself for the way he'd judged you falsely and that if he'd stayed and helped you, you might not have had to marry Riley Dawson," Pamela explained.

Zandy could not have been more surprised. "He came back here for me?"

"Yes," Pamela replied. She leaned back wearily and yawned. "He didn't know about Riley coming to God. He didn't even know you were living in Missouri. He just thought he'd come here and rescue you from your misery. You should have seen his face when I told him you and Riley were madly in love with one another. I even told him about the baby. But that was before—" she stopped suddenly.

"Before?" Zandy pressed.

"That was before so much. It's hard to believe that only a few weeks have passed. It seems like an eternity." Pamela sighed and looked away.

"Why don't you rest now?" Zandy said and started to leave.

"No! I have to tell you the rest. There's so much you don't know."

"All right, but you must sleep once you've finished."

"I will," Pamela promised. She hesitated for a moment and then began to tell the whole story of what happened after Jim realized he'd taken the wrong woman. Pamela stressed that he'd treated her with the utmost care, leaving out the time she had walked to exhaustion in the rain.

"Then the outlaws from the Owens gang took me. They told me that Jim was dead, and that's when Esther Owens, the leader, read about me in the Denver paper. Zandy, she was the one responsible for the ransom notes. She told me herself that she intended to make at least one million dollars out of my disappearance. She wanted to wire Mother and Father, but I told her she'd have better luck with you and Riley, only because I felt more confident that you and Riley could get me back alive."

"That's high praise, indeed," Zandy said with a bit of smile. The baby shifted, and Zandy grew uncomfortable in her awkward position on the side of the bed.

"I know that Uncle Bob believes that Jim was responsible for my kidnapping, and it is true that he took me at first, but only because he thought he was doing you a favor. Jim rescued me from the Owens gang. He risked his life with some drifter named Caleb something-or-other, and he was bringing me home when Uncle Bob's men found us. Zandy, you can't let him pay for this. Jim never intended me harm. He never intended anyone harm."

"I can believe that," Zandy replied quietly. She remembered Jim's kindness to her before he had lost faith in her virtue.

"Zandy, I prayed and prayed about all of this. I've been so stupid and foolish. Can you forgive me?" Pamela's declaration took Zandy off guard.

"What are you talking about?"

"Bradley has married someone else, a very rich woman in Kansas City. They are even now on their honeymoon in Europe, or so the paper tells."

"I'm sorry, Pamela."

"I was so hurt, Zandy. I thought I loved him, truly I did. But when I realized what had happened, I knew I was only agreeing to marry Bradley because it would hurt my parents as much as they'd hurt me. I knew their social standing was important to them. A great deal more important, I might add, than I was. I wanted to get their attention, and I wanted to make them pay. But now God has shown me that this isn't the way to be. I know nothing would ever have been resolved between us and maybe it still can't be, but at least I didn't marry a man I didn't love."

"God has a way of interceding," Zandy said. She smiled, remembering Riley's verse about intercession. "It's His way to keep up from hurting ourselves in our lack of knowledge and direction. He loves us very much, and even though it often seems He has rejected us, He never will. The Bible says He will always be with us."

"I believe that. Probably now more than before," Pamela admitted.

"That's because your faith has been tested. You have found it necessary to rely on God, not because I said He was good or because of what you saw Him do for Riley. You went to God with your own need and from that moment on, He worked through your faith to help you trust Him."

"It was the only comfort I had, but now I fear Uncle Bob will hang Jim before the truth is told. Zandy, will you please help me? Can you go to the jail and talk to Jim? We have to see what the sheriff plans and how soon we can free him."

"I don't know," Zandy said slowly. She knew Riley would never allow her to go into town, and she couldn't very well send Riley to appear on Jim's behalf. Not when Jim had planned to take her in the first place.

"Does Riley know that Jim planned to take me?" Zandy suddenly asked.

Pamela nodded. "He left a note. He didn't sign it, but he figured Riley would know it was him."

"I see," Zandy said. "That complicates matters even more, but I'll do what I can."

Pamela's look of worry lessened with her friend's promise of help. "Then I'll rest. We can talk more later, but there's one thing I have to know."

"What is it?" Zandy questioned.

"You will forgive me for putting you in the middle of all of this, won't you? I mean, I practically forced you to bring me to Colorado, and I was hideously overbearing back there in Missouri. And all of it was because I was such a spoiled child, but, Zandy," Pamela paused and sat up to take Zandy's hand, "I'm not that child anymore."

Zandy smiled and gave Pamela's hand a squeeze. "I know that, and of course I forgive you. Now get some sleep. I've got some planning to do."

ও

Zandy knew that in order to get to Jim, she'd have to leave the house unseen. This would be a difficult task, at best. Someone was always coming to see her about something, if for no other reason than to talk. Finally settling on saying nothing to anyone, Zandy slipped out the back door and made her way into town.

She moved slowly, cautious for the sake of her oversized stomach. She would have relished the comfort of a buggy, but she knew that sending for it would only draw immediate attention to her departure. Besides, she chided herself, the jail wasn't even half a mile away.

Since it was only midday, the town of Dawson was moderately quiet. There was the normal mining traffic with wagons of ore being hauled to processing and the scales. The train whistle blasted, startling Zandy for only a moment. Somehow she figured Riley's voice would closely resemble the same noise when he learned of her absence. Especially when he found out she'd gone to visit Jim Williams.

She pulled her shawl tight around her roomy brown calico dress and kept her head down and eyes to the boardwalk. She passed by several men who made suggestive comments about her condition, and even though her cheeks felt hot from their words, Zandy refused to acknowledge that she'd heard them at all.

Pushing open the door to the jail, Zandy lifted her face and met the eyes of K.C. Russell. Remembering K.C. as one of the deputies Riley had hired when he'd first come to Dawson, Zandy felt a little more confident in her mission.

"I've come to see Jim," she stated firmly.

K.C. eyed her suspiciously. "I can't let you do that Missus Dawson."

"I'm not leaving until I talk to him face to face," Zandy said with her hands planted firmly on her hips.

Just then Mike Muldair, another of the men Riley had hired for law and order in Dawson, appeared. "K.C., you'll be havin' to come help me!"

"What's the problem?" K.C. asked, momentarily forgetting about Zandy.

"It's that fool Jake Atkins and his brother Tom," Mike said, his Irish heritage betraying itself in his speech. "Jake's a wee bit in his cups if you know what I mean."

K.C. nodded. Everybody knew about Jake's drinking habits. "Well, the fool has gone and shot up the Red Lady Saloon, and now Tom is tryin' to keep him from shootin' the barkeep for denyin' him whiskey. We need to give ol' Tom a hand before he puts a bullet in Jake, himself."

K.C. moved to the door, then remembered Zandy. "I can't leave with her here."

Mike moved to help usher Zandy outside, but the sound of more gunshots sent him away from her and out the door. "Ferget the fool woman and come on. We'll be in for it with Tom if we don't help him corral that brother of his."

K.C. finally gave up worrying about Zandy and ran after Mike. Zandy thanked God for the reprieve. She opened the door that separated the cells from the office and called out, "Jim? Are you in here?"

The light was dim, but Zandy could see a man rise from the cot in his cell. "Zandy?"

"Yes," she answered, and came to stand directly in front of him. "Pamela begged me to help you, and I've come to do what I can." Jim looked tired, and Zandy couldn't help but feel sorry for him.

"You shouldn't be here," Jim replied. "I never wanted you to get involved in this."

"You involved me, or don't you remember?" Zandy questioned in a gentle tone.

"She told you?"

"Yes," Zandy replied. "I guess in a way I feel honored that you cared so much. I often wondered if you'd forgiven me for the wrongs you'd presumed me capable of."

"Me forgive you?" Jim laughed. "I think we both know it's the other way around. I need your forgiveness, Zandy. I wronged you something terrible, and I've had to live with it all this time. Even before Pat told me the truth of the matter, I knew down deep inside that you weren't capable of doing what I said you'd done."

"I forgive you, Jim."

"Just like that?" Jim questioned. "Even after all of this?"

"Just like that," Zandy replied. "If you had taken me, Jim and then found out I was content—in fact, happy— wouldn't you have brought me back home?"

"Of course."

"You tried to bring Pamela back home, too, and, as she tells it, it nearly cost you your life. I think I know that you never intended harm to anyone, and I will see to it that everyone else knows it as well. I'll find some way to get you out of here. Just don't give up."

Jim went back to the cot and slumped down in complete dejection. "There's no way they're gonna let me out of here. I've got no way to prove that anything I say is true. It's my word against theirs."

"And Pamela," Zandy insisted. "She seems really concerned. She was nearly hysterical trying to get someone to see reason. I think she cares a great deal what happens to you."

Jim crossed his arms and sighed. "It won't do any good if that uncle of hers is out for blood, like his men said. He's gonna find a tree and string me up. This whole thing is impossible."

"Nothing is impossible with Christ," Zandy said. "The Bible is clear on this matter. You must put your faith in God, Jim. He's your salvation in this situation, and He won't let you down. I'll be praying for you, and you must do the same. Remember, the Bible says in Matthew eighteen, verse twenty, 'For where two or three are gathered together in my name, there am I in the midst of them.' Between you, me, and Pamela praying, God will be with us, and He'll answer. He won't let you be falsely punished."

"I'd like to believe that," Jim said lifting his head.

"Then believe it. God won't let you bear this alone."

The words reminded Jim of what he'd himself said to Pamela when she'd learned of Bradley's marriage. He nodded slowly. He had to trust that it was true.

"All right, Zandy. I'll be praying."

sixteen

Zandy walked from the room with a new determination to free Jim. She noticed that K.C. was still absent from the office and breathed a sigh of relief that she'd not have to explain herself to anyone. Her relief was short-lived, however. She walked out the door of the jail and straight into the waiting arms of her husband.

"Riley!" she gasped. Looking into his angry face, Zandy steeled herself for his rage.

"Alexandra," he said between clenched teeth, "we need to talk." He took a firm grip on her arm and pulled her with him.

"I can explain, Riley."

"Oh, you will definitely do that," he replied, barely controlling his temper. "Starting with why you came into town when I left explicit orders that you were to stay in the house."

"I had to come. Pamela said that Jim is innocent of trying to get ransom for her. He was bringing her home, Riley."

"It still doesn't answer my question. I gave you orders for your own good. I didn't do it just so I could have the upper hand with you. This town isn't safe, and you know that full well. If you couldn't respect my wishes for your own safety, how dare you risk the life of our child!"

Zandy felt herself close to tears at his accusation. She was more angry than she'd ever been. "How could you, Riley? How could you?"

Riley stopped and looked into her angry green eyes. "I don't want to bury you. This town is out of control, and decent folk aren't safe. The sheriff spends his day running from one end of the town to another, just to identify the bodies. You knew the risk, yet you figured that man in there was worth more than your own life or your baby's."

Zandy raised her hand to slap Riley, then halted, suddenly realizing what she was about to do. Taking a deep breath, she pushed away, but Riley wouldn't let her go. Instead, he moved her toward the carriage he'd brought.

"Get in," he said, helping her up.

Zandy did as she was told. She was mortified that she'd been angry enough to hit her husband. What was wrong with her? She'd never in her life felt like this.

Riley quickly joined her and slapped the reins against the horse's backside. With a jerk the buggy moved down the street, and when Riley turned away from the road that would take them home, Zandy turned to question him.

"I thought I was supposed to be at home," she said in a sarcastic voice.

"We're going to talk about this first, and I don't need an audience," Riley replied. Once they were outside of the town proper, Riley directed the horse off the road and into a small clearing. Pulling back on the reins, Riley turned to face his wife. "I love you, Alexandra. I've tried to be a good husband, a proper husband, but you challenge me at every turn. How can I lead if you won't let me? We can't even face life side by side, because you continue to take matters into your own hands.

"You've insisted on interfering in things that aren't of your concern, and this time it could have well cost you your life. Pamela's problems are her own making, just as

Jim's are. You have to leave them alone to resolve the messes they've gotten themselves into."

"You don't even care that an innocent man may die," Zandy declared. Her eyes were ablaze with the fire of her anger. "Jim may be hanged because of something he didn't do. He never intended to kidnap Pamela."

"I know," Riley replied, matching her anger. "He intended to take you! Did you know that?"

Zandy sighed. She felt the baby move restlessly in her belly and wondered if she was causing her child harm by arguing with Riley. Finally, she nodded, and when she spoke, her tone was less harsh.

"Yes, I know. Pamela told me first, and Jim and I discussed it. Why didn't you tell me?"

Riley recognized that her anger had lessened. "I couldn't. I thought it might be Jim, but I couldn't be sure. The thought of anyone trying to take you from me, for any reason, left me cold. I didn't want you to worry and wonder, and that was one of the biggest reasons I insisted you stay in the house."

"But Jim didn't want to hurt me. He thought I was living in misery with you," Zandy stated.

"It doesn't matter what he thought!" Riley declared. He felt his rage burning high again. How dare any man think he could walk in and take another man's wife?

"It does!" Zandy exclaimed. "He didn't mean to hurt anyone."

"Well he did. Alexandra, you have to stay out of this." Riley's insistent tone caused Zandy's anger to rekindle.

"I can't!"

"You will or else!" Riley demanded.

"Or else what? Are you going to lock me in my room?"

"If I have to." Riley was nose to nose with her by this time.

Zandy clenched her fists in her lap. "Take me home."

"Not until you understand how things are going to be," Riley replied.

"God expects us to fight for the right," Zandy said. "He doesn't expect us to hide in fear just because something bad might happen. I know Jim is innocent, and you expect me to say and do nothing to try and stop an injustice being done. That's not of God! You simply can't forgive Jim for caring about my happiness. Forgiveness is a part of your responsibility as a child of God as well. Luke seventeen, verse three says, 'Take heed to yourselves: If thy brother trespass against thee, rebuke him; and if he repent, forgive him.' Jim asked my forgiveness and I gave it. You should learn to do the same."

Riley shook his head. There was no reasoning with her. She drew on her years of Bible teaching and verse memorization and used it like a mighty weapon against him. Taking the reins in hand, Riley urged the horse forward.

They said nothing on the way back to the house. When Riley stopped the horse just beyond the back entryway, Zandy climbed down awkwardly from the buggy and ran into the house.

Riley wanted to call out to her. He wanted to stop her and ease the anger between them, but he couldn't. He couldn't find a way to get past her consistently placing herself beyond his authority. He couldn't help her to see that he didn't want to dominate or rule her as a king would a subject, he just wanted to protect her and see to her safety and the safety of his child.

Inside the house, Zandy let go the tears she'd been

holding back. Why was she so angry when she knew that Riley was right? Maybe it was because he was right that she was mad. All her life, she'd tried to live by the Word of God, and now she almost hated herself for throwing it in Riley's face. She knew full well that wasn't the way God had intended it to be used.

Moving with weighted steps, Zandy felt as though a burden was crushing her down. She had never allowed there to be this kind of anger between her and Riley. How could she resolve it? How could she make him see that Jim's life was just as important and just as worth saving as her own?

She made her way to Pamela's room and knocked lightly.

"Come in," the voice called from within, and Zandy pushed back the door. Tears still streamed down her cheeks, and Pamela immediately took notice. "What is it, Zandy? Is Jim...is he...?"

"No, Jim is fine," Zandy said, getting control of her emotions. "I just had a horrible fight with Riley. He found out that I'd gone to the jail. He was livid, of course. Oh Pamela, I can't convince him that we need to fight Jim's cause. He just won't listen to reason."

Pamela nodded in complete understanding. "I know exactly how you feel. I tried to talk to my Uncle Bob, but he won't listen to reason either. I told him everything, including how Jim saved my life, but he just doesn't see that it merits helping him now. He says that Jim made those kind of choices when he decided to take me in the first place. Oh, Zandy. What are we going to do?"

"I don't know," Zandy replied in complete exasperation. There didn't seem to be any answer. Then her conversation with Jim slowly came back to her. "Yes, I do." Her words held more confidence. "We'll do exactly as I told

Jim to do. We'll pray. The three of us will pray for Jim's deliverance. There is a thing called intercession. Riley himself told me about it. It's a kind of coming before someone on someone else's behalf. Jesus intercedes for us, as does the Holy Spirit. Now we are going to intercede for Jim," Zandy replied confidently.

Pamela seemed to pick up on her enthusiasm. "Just tell me what I must do."

For a time, they prayed together. Then Zandy left Pamela and went to another of the empty bedrooms and locked the door. She had no desire to see Riley. Her heart was still filled with anger toward him, and it became very clear to her that it hindered her prayers.

"God," she prayed, getting to her knees beside the bed. "I've served You for so long and believed that Your Word was true. I know You have a purpose in this situation, yet I can't see what possible good can come from Jim's imprisonment. I feel so angry with my husband, because...." Zandy fell silent. Why was she mad at Riley?

"I don't know how to live with him," she finally said. A bit of a laugh came out, surprising Zandy. "I've been married to him for some time now, yet I still don't know how to be a good wife. He hasn't the years of spiritual training I've had, and I suppose that makes me feel like I have to lead him. But I don't, do I Lord?" It wasn't really a question, because Zandy already knew the answer.

"I don't need to lead him, because You will. But You can't help him if I'm always interfering. Forgive me, Father. I don't mean to be so foolish and blind. It's hard to follow Riley," she whispered. "It's hard, because I'm afraid he won't know what Your Will is on the matter. I suppose I've become a bit of a snob when it comes to my Christian teachings. I can't seem to accept that You can fill Riley with all the wisdom and knowledge he needs in order to be a good husband. Help me, Father. Help me to trust You to guide Riley. Help me to be a wife who is a helper, not a hinderer. I don't want to cause Riley to give up in discouragement."

Zandy immediately felt better. She could suddenly see how she had tried to lead the spiritual matters in their home for some time. It wasn't that Riley didn't want the responsibility, as was the situation for the husbands in some homes, it was that she wouldn't let him have it.

Getting up from the floor, Zandy sat on the bed and began to wonder how she could deal with the situation in a way that would put all the wrongs to right. She loved her husband, of this she had no doubt. But Jim was innocent, and someone had to convince Robert and Riley in order for him to go free.

"God, You are our only hope," Zandy whispered. "Please help Riley and Robert to see the truth, and help Pamela and me to leave it in Your hands. Amen."

seventeen

Robert Charbonneau stood amidst the men with a determined look on his face. Four of the original men he'd hired to find Pamela waited in silence for their temporary boss to speak. Robert sized each man up as the type who had no conscience and then proceeded with his plan.

"I find it necessary to call upon your assistance once again," Robert began. "My niece is creating quite a stir with stories of her ordeal. She's completely lost her sense in the matter and truly believes Jim Williams innocent of her abduction. Personally, I think it's just one of those addle-headed female infatuations, but I find it most impossible to persuade her otherwise.

"And, as you know," Robert continued, "our friend is still sitting in his jail cell awaiting some type of justice. I for one am growing weary of the wait. It's been four weeks, and I don't care how much flooding there's been, we're entitled to a speedy trial for this man. Whether a judge can get through the pass or not, I intend to see justice carried out swiftly."

"What are we supposed to do?" the leader of the group asked. He was a stout man with red hair that hadn't seen a washing in more than month of hard riding. He spat tobacco juice on the ground, and Robert was silently grateful that he'd decided to hold this meeting in the barn instead of the house.

"I'm sure we can think of something," Robert replied.

The man stared blankly for a moment then seemed to catch Charbonneau's meaning. "We can't very well hang him properly in his cell."

It was as he made this comment that Pamela came upon the men. They didn't see or hear her, so she crept into one of the empty stalls and listened.

"No, that's true," Robert said, thoughtfully rubbing his chin. "However, he could be shot trying to escape. Desperate folks attempt extreme measures when faced with the possibility of their own death. How hard would it be for a man to attempt such an escape?"

The red-headed man leered a grin. "Not hard at all with the proper kind of encouragement."

The stall was hot and dusty, and Pamela felt sweat pouring down her back. Still, she couldn't risk being seen and give away the fact that she knew what her uncle was planning.

"Well, gentlemen," Robert said with a satisfied smile, "I suggest we be about our business right away. This is Saturday, and Saturday nights in Dawson seem to be a most laborious night for our sheriff and his deputies. What say we plan a little diversion just in case the town rowdies don't accommodate us?"

"A fire would bring just about the whole town to help," one of the other men offered.

"A fire would be good," Robert said with a nod. "It must be threatening enough, without doing too much damage. After all, we wouldn't want the entire town destroyed."

"There's some old shacks down at the south end of town, just across Meiers Gulch," the leader remembered. "They're used for storing mining equipment and such. We could set those on fire, and with Corner Creek between it and town, it would bring folks to put out the fire, without risking the Main Street district."

"Good. Then that's what we'll do. Can you get enough help to set the fire and still have enough men to offer the encouragement needed for our friend to escape?" Robert asked, eyeing his watch. It was nearly five. "Say we set the fire around six. Then have things set up at the jail. Just in case you can't get the deputy to leave the place, have another man wait outside to announce some problem. Maybe you could tell him that someone was breaking into the assay office. Just use any old excuse to clear the jail."

"We can handle it, boss. When the money's right, we can do most anything we need to."

Robert laughed, "A man after my own heart."

Pamela shuddered to think that her uncle could so cold-heartedly plan the death of another. In the weeks since her return, while Jim waited in prison for the circuit judge, she'd only managed to slip notes to Jim by way of one of Zandy's brother's friends. He, of course, couldn't write back, but he usually gave the boy a message for her, and, though it often came to her in a most garbled fashion, Pamela knew that Jim was not giving up hope that God would send him a reprieve.

When the men departed for town and Robert hurried back to the mansion, Pamela made a dash for Zandy's room. Mindless of the straw that still clung to her skirt, she rushed up the back servants' stairs and knocked softly on the door.

Zandy opened the door, not at all surprised to find Pamela. "What is it?" she asked, however, when she saw the look of terror in her friend's eyes.

"Uncle Bob plans to kill Jim!" she exclaimed barely above a whisper.

Zandy motioned Pamela inside. She quickly closed and locked the door before pulling Pamela toward the far end of the room.

"No one will hear us if we talk softly," Zandy said.

Pamela stared for a moment, as if seeing her friend for the first time. Zandy was obviously very expectant and Pamela knew it would only be a matter of weeks before the baby would be born. How could she even begin to involve her in this mess?

"I'd better just handle this alone," Pamela finally spoke. "You aren't in any condition to be helping me, and there isn't time to get anyone else."

"What are you talking about?" Zandy questioned. She reached out to force Pamela to stay where she was.

"My uncle is planning a jailbreak for Jim. It's going to happen in just an hour or so. I overheard them talking in the barn. And, Zandy," Pamela said, with tears in her eyes, "they plan to kill him."

"No!" Zandy exclaimed louder than she'd intended.

"Uncle Bob is just convinced that I'm too stupid to see Jim for what he is. He thinks I wear my heart on my sleeve and give it to every man that comes along," Pamela explained. "Now, he's convinced that I'm lying to save Jim because I'm in love with him."

Zandy's eyes widened. "Are you, Pamela? Are you in love with Jim?"

"I don't know, Zandy. I care very much for him. He was so kind and gentle. Yet he was firm with me, too. He never once allowed that spoiled, little-girl attitude of mine to run the show. He made it clear that he'd not tolerate my selfishness, and I guess I needed that to show me what I'd truly become."

"But that's not the same as loving him. You must know whether or not you care that much," Zandy pressed.

Pamela put her hands to the sides of her head as if to press out the images that were flashing through her mind. She could easily see the plan her uncle made coming true. She could see Jim lying dead in the muddy street of Dawson.

"I've thought constantly of him since our return," Pamela admitted. "I've thought of the way he consoled me when we learned about Bradley. He was so tender, and yet he helped me to see God's hand in it all, and he made me understand that I didn't have to face my pain alone. I've slipped notes of encouragement to him on more than one occasion, but the message I get back is never one that shows anything more than curt acknowledgement of having received them."

"What do you expect, love letters?" Zandy asked with a smile. "You need to listen to that heart's calling you're always talking about. I think if you listen long enough, you'll find that you care more about Jim than you're willing to admit."

Pamela nodded, then paled when she heard the clock chiming half-past the hour. "We've only got a little less than half an hour. They plan to set some shacks on fire to create a diversion on the opposite side of town!" Pamela exclaimed. She pulled away from Zandy and hurried to the door. "Is Riley back yet?"

Zandy shook her head. "His meeting with Mister Tabor must have lasted longer than he planned. He wired to say he'd arrive on this evening's train."

"Then he can't very well help us," Pamela replied, and fumbled to unlock the door. "What about your parents?"

"They're out visiting friends, and I don't know when

they'll be back," Zandy answered, and crossed the room. "Look, whether you like it or not, you're stuck with me. They won't threaten Jim if we're there. I mean, how would it look? A respectable young woman and a mother-to-be standing between them and their man. What are they going to do, shoot us?"

"They very well could, Zandy. That's why I don't want you to come with me."

"Nonsense," Zandy replied. "You run ahead and make certain your uncle isn't going to see us leave. I'll be downstairs directly and meet you at the back door." Pamela nodded reluctantly and hurried to do what Zandy suggested.

After a hurried prayer for guidance, the two women slipped into the dusky shadows of twilight. Zandy directed Pamela to take the garden path, for the extra coverage of the shrubbery and vegetation. The lingering scent of flowers and pine lent the lavender sky an air of romance, but the thoughts in the minds of Zandy and Pamela were far from that pleasure.

Dawson was already enjoying an over-zealous celebration for the week's end of work. The last shift at the mine was just finishing, and Zandy knew that six o'clock would be signaled by the explosion that would be set off to blast ore from the rock face of the mines. She knew they would need to be in place at the jail before that, and she hurried, in spite of her cumbersome burden, to keep pace with Pamela's lithe and graceful form. They had to make it time. They just had to!

❧

A hot and exhausted Riley Dawson stepped from the five-forty-five train. He glanced at his house up on the hill and sighed in relief to know that very soon it would be Horace Tabor's problem to contend with. The sounds of gunshots and laughter from the brothel and gambling districts hurried his step toward the sanity and safety of his home.

His mind had been greatly preoccupied with thoughts of Zandy. There was so much that needed to be said between them, and he wanted very much to put an end to her worries about Jim. But how? How could he get Zandy to see reason where Jim was concerned? She cared too much, and that bothered Riley more than he could say. Was it possible that Zandy cared more for Jim than she was letting on? It was something that Riley had to find out. He had to know why she was so persistent in defending him.

The walk did him good and helped Riley to clear his head. He was glad to be home, yet completely reluctant to deal with his wife. "God," he breathed the prayer, "give me the guidance I need to do what I must. Let my words be carefully chosen, and please let Zandy speak honestly to me."

The house greeted him in silence, and Riley couldn't shake off the feeling that something was wrong.

"Zandy!" he called out as he took the stairs two at a time. Their bedroom revealed nothing. Perhaps she was spending time with Pamela.

Riley walked quickly to the end of the hall where Pamela's room was. He knocked loudly and when no one answered, he opened the door. Nothing!

Now Riley was worried. He hurried back downstairs and nearly ran through each room, trying to locate the women. When he reached the library a single cough let him know the room was occupied.

"Robert?" he questioned, coming into the room.

"I see you made it back," Robert replied from where he sat.

"Have you seen the women?"

Robert shook his head, noting the worried expression on Riley's face. "Not since this afternoon. After lunch, Zandy went to take a nap and Pamela went to her room. Why?"

"They aren't in the house, and I didn't see them on the grounds when I came home. I'm going to check the gardens, but as dark as it's getting, they both know better than to be out there. Where are Burley and Ruth and the kids?" Riley called out from the doorway.

"I don't know," Robert said. He was completely confused as to why Riley was so disturbed. "I wouldn't worry too much, Riley. They're probably just off sewing for the baby or some such thing. I've not seen them leave the house all day, and I've been here the whole time."

Riley ignored the man's assurance. He knew how determined his wife could be if she felt the need to see to some matter. A quick examination of the gardens revealed them to be as empty as the bedrooms had been.

Riley ran a hand through his sweat-soaked hair and returned to the house. Where were they?

Coming back to the library, Riley heard the clock chime six. This was followed by the rocking explosion that signaled the end of the mining shift. Robert glanced up and started to speak, but Riley's look silenced him.

"If they aren't here, there's only one place I can imagine the two of them would have gone," Riley stated. "They must have gone to the jail to see Williams."

Robert paled and got to his feet. "They wouldn't! They couldn't have. I would have seen them leave."

"Be realistic, Charbonneau. Those two are fully capable of giving you the slip if they so choose. They aren't here, so that means they must be somewhere. My guess is the jail."

Robert glanced at the clock and back to Riley. The look on his face changed from calm to anguished. "They can't be at the jail."

"Why not?" Riley said, coming forward. "What is it that you're not telling me, Robert?"

"I...well, you see, I—"

"What is it, man? If you know something that can help me find them, you'd best tell me now," Riley said, nearly taking hold of Robert.

"I arranged for Williams to escape from the jail. I set it up so he'd be shot, and we'd be free once and for all without having to wait for a judge to hang him!"

Riley felt the color drain from his own face. He wanted to wring Charbonneau's neck, but that wouldn't change a thing.

"When?" Riley questioned, throwing Robert a murderous look.

"Right now," Robert answered.

Riley didn't say another word. He could only offer up a prayer while running at desperate pace to reach the jail before Robert's plan could be executed.

eighteen

When Zandy and Pamela arrived at the jail, it was empty. Fearing that somehow the hired thugs had already coerced Jim from the cell, Zandy rushed through the office as fast as she could.

"Jim!" she called, stumbling through the darkness.

"Zandy? What are you doing here?" Jim questioned from his cell.

"Oh, Jim!" Pamela exclaimed, coming behind Zandy. "They plan to kill you. I heard them talk, and they're going to stage a jail-break and shoot you while you run."

"Pamela?" Jim's voice revealed his surprise. "You two shouldn't be here, especially if what you say is true."

Pamela came to the cell where Jim stood. She could barely see his face in the fading light. "We had to come. We had to warn you, and see if we couldn't stop it. My uncle won't listen to reason. I've tried to explain the matter to him over and over again, but he won't listen. Now there isn't time to go for help. He and his men planned for the jail to be empty except for you."

"Look, you and Zandy have to go back to the safety of the house. I can take care of myself, and we have to trust God to look out for me as well. I'm not running anymore. The last time I did, I ended up causing more hurt and trouble than it was worth."

Zandy stepped forward at this. "Jim, the past has been resolved. I forgive you, now you must forgive yourself.

You have a great deal to live for, and I won't see you putting yourself into the hands of those madmen."

"Forgiving is the easy part," Jim said softly. "The forgetting is a whole heap harder."

"We haven't got time to worry about it just now," Zandy said firmly. "They mean to show up here any minute."

Pamela turned to Zandy. "Would you mind giving me a minute alone with Jim? I think I can convince him that we need to help him."

"I'll be just outside," Zandy said with quick squeeze of Pamela's hand. "I'll keep watch."

Pamela waited until Zandy had closed the door before she spoke again. "Jim, I've got to say something to you, and you've got to listen to me carefully. I can't stand by and watch them kill you. I've come to care too much about you." She paused for a moment, wishing she could better see his face. Stepping closer to the bars, Pamela was surprised when Jim's hands reached out to touch her arms.

"I care about you, too," Jim remarked. "That's why I don't want you here."

"But I can't leave!" Pamela exclaimed. "I love you!"

The silence that fell between them caused Pamela to fear Jim would reject her feelings. He knew her foolishness over Bradley. Perhaps he'd give her declaration no consideration at all.

"Did you hear me?" she finally managed to whisper.

"Yes," he replied. "I love you, too."

"You do?" Pamela questioned leaning forward against the bars. Jim slipped his arms around her as best he could.

"I've loved you for a while now. I guess I was just waiting for you to heed the heart's calling, as you'd put it."

Pamela pressed her face to his.

"Yes, I suppose that's it," she whispered.

Just then, Zandy came back and slammed the door closed. "Something's happening out there!" she exclaimed, and surprised both Pamela and Jim by pulling a small revolver from her skirt pocket.

"Zandy!" Pamela cried, and moved to her friend. "You can't mean to use that."

"I'll do what I must to keep them from killing Jim. He doesn't deserve to die in a shoot-out." Zandy strained her eyes in the dim light to see if there was anything she could use to keep the ruffians from entering.

"Look," Pamela said, and reached up to a small bolt on the door. She quickly slid the lock into place.

"I don't remember that being there," Zandy said, breathing a sigh. "It won't keep them out, but it will slow them down. Now Pamela, you get back in the corner by Jim."

"Zandy you've got to stop this," Jim said, to no avail. "You can't risk your life and your child's for me. I'm perfectly willing to put my life in God's hands."

"That's where all of us are at the moment, Jim," Zandy countered. "You can't protect yourself in there, so I'm just doing what I feel I must. You'd do no different if it were me or Pamela in there and you out here."

"But that's different," Jim protested.

Just then shouting from outside the jail could be heard. The ruckus grew until several shots were exchanged. Zandy began to tremble. On the other side of the door, she could hear men's voices. She slowly backed up against the bars of an empty cell and leveled the gun at the door.

The latch was tried, and, when the door wouldn't budge, Zandy, Pamela, and Jim could hear someone kicking against it. These outlaws would beat the door down, Zandy realized, and then she'd have to face them. Could she do it? Could she actually take a life in order to save one? For the first time, she questioned the sanity of what she was doing. If Riley found out, he'd be furious. Smothered in guilt, Zandy waited for the inevitable.

The door gave in with a resounding crash and from the doorway rose the shadowy figure of a man. Zandy lifted the revolver higher.

"Stop or I'll shoot," she said in a shaky voice.

"Alexandra!"

It was Riley. She'd nearly shot her own husband! Sickened from the entire episode, Zandy lowered her arm as her knees gave way.

Riley stepped into the room, secured the gun, and lifted Zandy into his arms. She shook so hard that her teeth chattered loudly.

"Are you hurt?" he questioned.

Robert rushed in behind him. "Are they all right? Where's Pamela?"

"I'm here Uncle Bob, and I'm fine. I just couldn't let you put an end to Jim's life. I love him, and I won't let you hurt him. He's not responsible for those ransom notes," Pamela said firmly. She stepped forward putting herself between Robert and Jim.

Robert studied Pamela for a moment, then shook his head. Turning, he saw that Riley was leaving with Zandy. "Is she all right?"

"I don't honestly know," Riley replied. "It's the first time I've found her speechless and the only time I've ever wished she'd rant and rave at me, if nothing else."

"I'm not hurt," Zandy managed to say and then added, "Just scared half-witless."

"Good," Riley retorted. "You deserve to be."

Just then the sheriff returned, having just found several men tied up and face down in the dirt outside his office. "What's going on in here?" he questioned, lighting a lantern. Turning up the light, he was surprised to find his jail so full of visitors.

Riley exited the cell room and deposited Zandy onto a chair with the order to stay put or else. Pamela quickly followed her uncle into the office, while Jim was forced to wait it out in the cell.

"I'm afraid you had a little problem here tonight," Riley said.

The sheriff snorted in disgust. "I've had a little problem all over town tonight, Mister Dawson. I'm afraid you're going to have to get yourself another sheriff. I quit."

"You can't!" Pamela exclaimed. "There are those who intend to see Jim Williams hang, and I'm here to tell you that he's not the man responsible for my kidnapping. He didn't send those ransom notes, and I will not be a part of any scheme to see him charged with such nonsense."

"Ma'am, by your own admission, Williams is the man who took you from the Dawson grounds," the sheriff replied.

"That's true, but it was a mistake, and there were no hard feelings between us. He was bringing me back when I was taken by the Owens gang. You have to believe me!" Pamela pleaded. "Please, Uncle Bob, I know what I'm saying. I'm not addlebrained."

"That's for sure!" a voice called out from the open doorway.

"Caleb!" Pamela exclaimed.

"Hello there, Little Bitty Gal," he said, with a smile

broader than Corner Creek during a spring flood. "Good to see you lookin' so well. What's all this about, Jim?"

"Oh, Caleb," Pamela said and moved across to pull the man by the arm. "They mean to hang Jim because they think he's responsible for my kidnapping. You know the truth. Please tell them!"

The sheriff eyed Caleb suspiciously. "Who's this?"

"He's Caleb Emerson," Pamela said, suddenly remembering his last name. "He was drifting through the area when Jim and I ran into trouble. He helped Jim after the Owens gang nearly killed him. When they took me, Caleb helped Jim rescue me."

"That true?" the sheriff questioned.

"All but the part about me drifting through," Caleb said. He opened his worn out vest to reveal a badge. "I'm a U.S. Marshall. Been after the Owens gang for some time now. Just happened that when they took Little Bitty here, I was around to help get her back. Old Jim was in pretty poor shape for several days, and I had to fight him down to keep him from stumblin' after her and bleedin' to death in the process."

Pamela's mouth dropped open at Caleb's declaration. "You're a marshall?"

Caleb laughed. "Yup. I'd been stakin' out the Owens gang for some time. That's how I knew about their hideout."

"Then Williams is truly innocent?" Robert questioned, looking first at his niece and then at Emerson.

"He sure is," Caleb confirmed. "In fact, he risked his life to go down into the box canyon the Owens gang used and pull this gal to safety."

Robert shook his head. "I thought for sure...." His words

died out. He'd nearly caused the death of an innocent man because of his unwillingness to believe Pamela's story.

"Given the fact that the marshall here is backing up Williams' story, I'll have to let him go," the sheriff told Robert.

"Of course," he replied. "I'll drop everything."

"Well that's all fine and dandy, but you and me have a bit of business to settle, if I'm not mistaken," the sheriff said.

"You'd better clear out your cells, 'cause you've got more company than you'd figured on," Caleb stated. "I've brought in what's left of the Owens gang. You're gonna have to jail 'em for me until I can make arrangements to take them to Denver."

Pamela looked up at Caleb and swallowed hard. "They're here? Outside?"

"Yup, but don't you worry," Caleb added with a smile. "I've got 'em wrapped up prettier than Christmas presents. They aren't gonna be any problem for you." With that, he went to see to his prisoners.

The sheriff, in turn, went in to release Jim while Riley turned to speak to Robert. "Your hot-headed stupidity nearly got my wife and your niece killed. That same shoot-first attitude is what's wrong with this entire town. I'm going to be mighty glad to be rid of it." He moved to retrieve Zandy, when Robert reached out and touched his sleeve.

"I'm sorry, Riley. I truly am. I know I'm to blame for this, and I intend to take my due. I'd have never seen either of the women placed in danger. You have to believe me."

Riley nodded, but the look of disgust still lined his features. Just then, Jim stepped into room and, in spite of his bedraggled condition, Pamela thought him the handsomest man in the world. She threw herself into his arms.

"Oh Jim," she cried, burying her face against his chest. "God did it. He sent the miracle we needed."

"I heard, Little Bitty Gal," he said with a laugh. Pamela pulled back at his use of Caleb's nickname and joined his laughter.

Riley lifted Zandy in his arms, in spite of her protest, and started to leave. He turned to face Jim for the first time, and, swallowing his pride, he spoke. "Williams, I want to see you at the house. There's a room for you there, and I think it would do us all good to have a long talk."

Jim nodded, knowing in his heart that he still needed to reconcile with Riley. "I'll be there."

Riley turned his face to Zandy and smiled. "Of course, first, I'm going to have a long talk with this young lady about wifely obedience and what I intend to do should she decide to go gunning for outlaws again."

At this, everyone but Zandy laughed. Zandy bit her lip and tried to ignore the look in Riley's eyes. It was the same kind of look that she'd seen some years earlier when he'd told Zandy he intended to be a part of her life forever. It was such a look of determination that it left Zandy in little doubt as to just who would have his way in the future.

Riley passed Caleb just outside the door. He was startled to find that one of the marshall's prisoners was a woman. A rather beautiful woman, at that.

Caleb pushed Esther Owens and her two remaining co-horts through the door to the sheriff's office. The men Riley and Robert had tied and left in the dirt were quickly retrieved by the sheriff himself, making the small jail office rather crowded.

Esther gave Pamela a curt nod of acknowledgement, and Pamela couldn't help but feel sorry for the woman. She'd treated her well during her captivity and, in all truth, Pamela couldn't really bring herself to hate the woman. Perhaps, in another time and situation, they might even have been friends.

Robert turned and met the gray-blue eyes of Esther Owens. For a moment there was a flash of recognition in his eyes, before he shook his head, thinking he was mistaken. Esther only smiled and moved into the cell to which Caleb guided her.

When Caleb had secured his prisoners, he returned to greet Jim. "Sure good to see that you're staying out of trouble, son," he said with a smile.

Jim extended his hand and gave Caleb's a hearty shake. "I can't thank you enough for all you've done. You were my answer to prayer."

"God does work in strange ways," Caleb replied, "but I don't recall anyone, save my wife, ever saying I was an answer to prayer."

"Well you are," Jim reaffirmed. "I don't know how to repay you."

"Just take care of that little bitty gal and stay close to the Lord. That'll be thanks enough," Caleb said with a laugh.

Jim grinned from ear to ear. "I intend to make that little bitty gal my wife. That is, if she'll have me."

All eyes, including Robert's, turned to Pamela. Pamela squealed in surprise and threw herself into Jim's arms. "Of course I'll have you!"

Jim looked over Pamela's head at Caleb. "I kind of thought she would," he said with a laugh.

nineteen

A long, hot August gave Jim and Pamela many fine days in which to get to know one another better. It seemed as though their close calls with death had produced changes and maturity in each of them that made all their old problems seem unimportant.

Three days before Jim and Pamela's September wedding, Riley signed the final papers that would give Horace Tabor ownership over all his holdings in Dawson. He felt much as if a weight had been lifted from his shoulders.

Zandy, finding her movements greatly restricted, was growing restless to bring her child into the world. Even so, she gave her best efforts to help with Pamela's wedding plans, fussing over the blond young beauty as though she were her own daughter.

Horace Tabor had agreed to wait until the end of the month before the actual transfer of property would take place. Riley had insisted on this due to his concern that Zandy would need time after the baby's birth to rest before she could travel back to Missouri. It also allowed for Pamela to have her wedding in the mansion, something that seemed to give Zandy a great amount of pleasure.

When the wedding day finally appeared, and the house had been decorated from top to bottom with orange blossoms, orchids, and ribbons, Zandy stood at Pamela's side and helped her to place the wedding veil on her carefully pinned and curled hair.

"You make a radiant bride, Pamela. I'm sure I've never seen another who could rival you."

"I'm so nervous. I'm afraid I'll pass out on the stairs," Pamela admitted.

"Nonsense," Zandy said with assurance. "I made it through my wedding under considerably more pressure and tension than you'll have. I never fainted once, although I felt like I might. You'll do fine. Now let me look at you and make sure everything is perfect."

Zandy stepped back, her emerald green, high-waisted gown rustling softly as she walked. She appraised Pamela's appearance for any flaw and found none. Her wedding gown was elaborate and completely current with the latest fashion. In a gesture that surprised everyone, Pamela's parents had arranged for the dress to be shipped from Paris, using Pamela's measurements to place the order. Even more surprising was their acceptance of her marriage to Jim, even though they declined to attend the wedding. They were, after all, invited to share company with a visiting Viscount and could not tear themselves away.

Zandy knew that Pamela was hurt at her parents' absence. She had confided in Zandy that the only reason they weren't making a fuss about her marriage was that Robert wholeheartedly approved of Jim as a husband. It seemed that after many hours of conversation, Jim and Robert had put aside their differences. Robert had even agreed to help Jim get established in some type of business, and, in a bizarre stroke of fate, they had become the best of friends.

Studying the silk gown trimmed in Brussels lace, Zandy could only smile her approval. "You look beautiful. I can't imagine a more perfect bride."

"You don't think the gown is too much?" Pamela asked,

suddenly fearful that she was unreasonably overdressed for such a small wedding.

"Never!" Zandy declared. She reached out and smoothed one of the many satin bows that trimmed the collar of the dress. "A bride can never be wrong in what she chooses to wear. It is her wedding, after all. Now turn around and let me make sure that the train is lying properly over the bustle."

Pamela turned and Zandy ran a careful hand beneath the veil to straighten the lace cap of the silk overdress. "There! Now it's perfect!" proclaimed Zandy, arranging the veil to fall gracefully behind the bride. "Now, where are your flowers?"

"Over there," Pamela replied, pointing, and she took a deep breath.

Zandy brought the bouquet to Pamela then turned her to the cheval mirror. "See for yourself."

Pamela moved to the mirror and gasped. The woman staring back couldn't possibly be her. "Oh," she whispered in awe.

"My thoughts exactly," Zandy said. She put a supportive hand to her back. Her burden was daily growing more uncomfortable.

Just then a knock sounded, and Pamela's uncle announced that it was time to come down. Zandy opened the door, and Robert, in his resplendent morning suit of dove gray, entered the room to admire his niece.

"Pammy, you look smashing!" he exclaimed.

Pamela beamed under his attention. "I'm so glad I have you to give me away. Mother and Father," she nearly choked on the words, "have never cared for me like you have." She moved to her uncle, lifted her veil, and bestowed a kiss upon his cheek. "I shall always love you for all that you've done."

Robert offered Pamela his arm, and Zandy hurried ahead of them. "You realize," Zandy stated at the top of the stairs, "you will have to give me ample time to descend as gracefully as this child will allow. That could very well take hours," she teased.

Pamela smiled and shook her head. "Jim and I have a lifetime, thanks to all of you. Take your time."

Zandy nodded and, in spite of the pain that tightened her abdomen, she smiled sweetly and gripped the banister for support. She wasn't about to spoil Pamela's day by announcing that she'd just had her first contraction.

In the large, front, morning room, Jim and Riley waited beside a short, balding man whose flowing black robe marked him as the preacher. Pastor Brokamp smiled broadly as Zandy appeared in the archway.

Zandy looked across the room to where Riley stood beside Jim. Both men were handsomely dressed in black claw hammer tail coats, with silk waistcoats and gray striped pants. She couldn't help but smile at the natural way Riley wore the clothes, in contrast to the most uncomfortable-looking Jim. She was grateful that Jim and Riley had put aside their differences to such a degree that Jim had asked Riley to stand up with him at the wedding.

Riley had easily forgiven Jim when he pointed out that someone as precious as Zandy deserved to have folks looking out after her happiness. Riley had realized then that Jim's only concern hadn't been for himself, but for Alexandra.

Burley, Ruth, and their children were the only other people in attendance. Both Jim and Pamela had hoped Caleb could attend, but he'd made it clear that his marshaling duties wouldn't permit the break. He promised to be there in spirit, however, and expressed happiness that the young folks were tying the knot. Taking her place across from the gentlemen, Zandy joined the others in watching Pamela process forward.

Pamela felt her legs shake and wondered if she could make it all the way to where the preacher waited with Jim. A part of her wished they'd just eloped while another part reveled in her special moment.

Jim's face bestowed a look of radiant approval as their eyes met and locked. Pamela felt strengthened just knowing that she'd take his arm at the end of the short walk. Jim had always given her a feeling of security, and today was no different.

Coming to stand in front of Pastor Brokamp, Robert presented Pamela's small hand to Jim. Jim stared down at Pamela through the veil and winked at her. Pamela couldn't help but smile. Soon, he'd be hers for all time.

The ceremony was short and simple, for which Zandy was most grateful. She stood without a word or movement through four very painful contractions. They were coming closer together, and Zandy remembered from the times her stepmother had given birth that the closer the contractions came, the sooner the baby would be born.

"You may kiss your bride," Pastor Brokamp said, and Jim lost little time in lifting Pamela's veil to do just that.

Everyone in the room rushed to congratulate the couple. The boys were laughing and shouting, while Molly squirmed out of Ruth's arms and ran to the various decorative flowers to pick her choices from the arrangements.

The cook and housekeeper appeared, bringing in two

large serving carts. One boasted a two-tiered wedding cake, and the other held a silver punch bowl and glasses.

"Oh boy, cake!" George declared and made his move to be one of the first to be served.

Riley was speaking to Robert when he happened to glance up and see Zandy's contorted face. She quickly turned to hide the pain she was feeling and tried to appear as though she were interested in the lace that edged her neckline. With one hand clamped securely against her stomach, Zandy waited for the pain to pass and nearly jumped out of her skin when Riley whispered against her ear.

"Are you all right?" he asked.

"I'm fine," Zandy replied. She nearly gasped from the intensity of the pain.

Riley tried to turn her to face him, but Zandy couldn't move. "Please, wait a minute." Her voice held an unmistakable tone of pain.

Riley took his hand from her shoulder and moved to face his wife. "What is it?"

"The baby," Zandy whispered. Just then, her water broke and hiding the fact that she was in labor became impossible. "I'm sorry!" she gasped and gripped Riley's arm for support.

Riley stared dumbly for a moment. Then a grin spread across his face. "I'm going to be a father," he announced, lifting Zandy in his arms. The children were oblivious to his announcement, while six adults, including the cook and housekeeper, dropped open their mouths in surprise.

Zandy winced against the pain, while Riley laughed, "Leave it to Alexandra to upstage the wedding."

"Oh, Pamela," Zandy moaned from her husband's arms. "I'm so sorry."

"Please, Zandy, don't be. This is a wonderful thing. I'll always remember my wedding as being the birthday of your first baby," Pamela reassured her. "But what can I do to help?"

Riley glanced at Ruth with a helpless look on his face. Zandy's stepmother recognized the need and instantly organized everyone into their appointed duties.

"Boys, take your little sister to the playroom and keep her occupied. Stay there, and I'll have cake and punch brought to you. Burley, go for the doctor. Riley, come with me. We'll get Zandy to bed."

Pamela, Jim, and Robert stood by helplessly while everyone else seemed to have some task to busy themselves with.

"I think I'd like to change my clothes," Jim announced.

Pamela hated to put aside her wedding finery, but knew she'd be of no help to anyone dressed as she was. She blushed slightly and followed Jim upstairs. Robert trailed after the couple and, finding nothing better to do, took himself to his own room to change.

Some minutes later, when everyone hurriedly reappeared in the hallway, they found Riley nervously pacing outside his own room.

"Ruth told me to wait out here," he said with a sheepish smile. "I told her I thought I ought to stay with Alexandra, but she said I'd done enough already."

Robert and Jim laughed and pulled Riley along with them. "Let's go downstairs and wait this out together." Riley threw a glance back over his shoulder, but Pamela only waved him on.

"She'll be just fine, Riley. I'll let you know the minute the baby comes," Pamela reassured him.

Throughout the day, Pamela moved back and forth from Zandy's bedside to the waiting men below. She gave what little help she could in the way of reports, and she finally convinced Robert and Jim to get Riley into some more comfortable clothes.

"All my clothes are in our room," Riley announced with an upward glance.

"I'll bring you whatever you want," Pamela said. "Just tell me where to find them."

All four of them progressed up the stairs, with Riley trying to remember where he'd put the things he wanted. Pamela finally directed Robert to take Riley to his room with the promise that she'd find the needed articles and return to them there.

She had just reached out to open the door when the unmistakable cry of a baby rang out, filling the hall. Riley blanched slightly, while Jim and Robert let out a whoop.

Pamela went into the room only long enough to make certain nothing was amiss.

"It's a boy, Riley!" she announced, coming back out. "You have a son, and Zandy is just fine."

Riley moved to the door, but Pamela put out her hand. "They aren't ready for you yet. So just relax. I'll call you when you can see them."

Riley turned to face his friends. A broad smile parted his lips to show his perfect teeth. "I told you," he laughed. "I told you it would be a boy!"

Ruth saw the doctor out, while Pamela stayed with Zandy. She smiled over the downy-headed child at his new mother. "He's a beautiful baby," Pamela declared.

Zandy nodded in complete awe. It was hard to believe something so perfect and tiny could be a part of her and

Riley's love for each other.

"I want to apologize to you," Pamela added, getting to her feet. "Looking at him, I can't believe I could have ever been so thoughtless as to endanger your life, much less his. Please forgive me."

Zandy looked up in surprise. "There's nothing to forgive. I did what I had to do. I'd do it again."

Pamela nodded. "I know what you mean. It's just that you and Riley have come to mean so much to me. I can't believe all of the trouble I've put you through. In so many ways I could have been responsible for driving a wedge between you."

Zandy shook her head. "No, the only walls that could come between us are the ones we put up ourselves. Riley and I are learning, just like you and Jim will learn, that marriage is a great deal of work and compromise." She snuggled her sleeping baby close and added with a nod, "But, it's very much worth the effort."

Pamela touched the tiny boy's head. "I'll keep that in mind. And you remember that, should you ever need anything, I am your dearest friend, forever."

"I'll remember," Zandy assured her.

Just then the door opened and admitted a proud Riley. He marched into the room as though he were taking charge of a meeting, and Pamela quickly made an excuse to depart. Standing for only a moment at the door, Pamela couldn't help but feel her heart flutter at the loving look on Riley's face as he reached out to take hold of his son. Someday, she'd give Jim a son and maybe even a daughter.

With a light heart, Pamela nearly danced out into the hall and fell headlong into the arms of her husband.

"Ummm," she sighed, as he bent his head to hers. "Don't

I know you?"

"I should hope so," he replied, and kissed her soundly.

Pamela threw her arms around her husband's neck. "I'm glad you kidnapped me," she declared. Jim only laughed.

"I know I'd have never given up my selfish, little-girl ideals if you hadn't come along to offer a little direction and guidance," she stated honestly. "I could never see how immature I truly was. Now that I have, I hope never again to be so self-centered."

"That makes two of us," Jim teased.

Pamela pushed her husband away and turned as if to walk off. "I bare my heart and soul, and you insult me. Maybe you should just go on the honeymoon by yourself." She'd only taken three steps when Jim crossed the distance, seized her abruptly, and threw her over his shoulder. Pamela giggled loudly, pleased with the turn of events.

"This kidnapping thing could get to be a habit," Jim announced, marching down the hall. "I guess a body just has to listen to the heart's calling in order to know what's best to do. Mine tells me I'm in for quite a life with you, Little Bitty Gal."

A Letter To Our Readers

Dear Reader:

In order that we might better contribute to your reading enjoyment, we would appreciate your taking a few minutes to respond to the following questions. When completed, please return to the following:

Rebecca Germany, Editor
Heartsong Presents
P.O. Box 719
Uhrichsville, Ohio 44683

1. Did you enjoy reading *The Heart's Calling*?
   ❏ Very much. I would like to see more books
      by this author!
   ❏ Moderately
      I would have enjoyed it more if _____

   _____

2. Are you a member of *Heartsong Presents*? Yes   No
   If no, where did you purchase this book? _____

   _____

3. What influenced your decision to purchase this
   book? (Check those that apply.)

   ❏ Cover   ❏ Back cover copy

   ❏ Title   ❏ Friends

   ❏ Publicity   ❏ Other _____

4. On a scale from 1 (poor) to 10 (superior), please rate the following elements.

___Heroine   ___Plot

___Hero   ___Inspirational theme

___Setting   ___Secondary characters

5. What settings would you like to see covered in *Heartsong Presents* books?

_____

_____

6. What are some inspirational themes you would like to see treated in future books?_____

_____

_____

7. Would you be interested in reading other *Heartsong Presents* titles? ☐ Yes   ☐ No

8. Please check your age range:
☐ Under 18   ☐ 18-24   ☐ 25-34
☐ 35-45   ☐ 46-55   ☐ Over 55

9. How many hours per week do you read? _____

Name _____

Occupation _____

Address _____

City _____ State _____ Zip _____

Frontiers of Faith

Kay Cornelius

___*Sign of the Bow*—Hours after the first warning of trouble, Sara Craighead, surrounded by Seneca warriors, is on a forced march through the dense woods. Her little brother was kidnapped by another group of Seneca, and Sarah has no idea whether her parents are dead or alive. HP87 $2.95

___*Sign of the Eagle*—Young and strong, Adam leaves his wilderness home to discover what work God has called him to. Adam's long blond hair and buckskin clothing cut a dashing figure on Philadelphia's streets and attract attention from two of the most eligible young women in the city. HP91 $2.95

___*Sign of the Dove*—As the end of war returns peace to Carolina, Hannah finds herself fighting a new battle in her heart. Not only must she determine her true feelings for Clay and Nate, but she also must resolve the anger and bitterness she harbors toward her cousin Marie. HP95 $2.95

___*Sign of the Spirit*—Coming Soon!

··· Hearts ♥ong ···

······ Presents ······

Great Inspirational Romance at a Great Price!

Heartsong Presents books are inspirational romances in contemporary and historical settings, designed to give you an enjoyable, spirit-lifting reading experience. You can choose from 116 wonderfully written titles from some of today's best authors like Colleen L. Reece, Brenda Bancroft, Janelle Jamison, and many others.

When ordering quantities less than twelve, above titles are $2.95 each.

SEND TO: Heartsong Presents Reader's Service
P.O. Box 719, Uhrichsville, Ohio 44683

Please send me the items checked above. I am enclosing $_____.
(please add $1.00 to cover postage per order. OH add 6.25% tax. NJ add 6%.). Send check or money order, no cash or C.O.D.s, please.
To place a credit card order, call 1-800-847-8270.

NAME _____

ADDRESS _____

CITY/STATE _____ ZIP _____

HPS MARCH

Hearts*♥*ng Presents
Love Stories Are Rated G!

That's for godly, gratifying, and of course, great! If you love a thrilling love story, but don't appreciate the sordidness of popular paperback romances, **Heartsong Presents** is for you. In fact, **Heartsong Presents** is the *only inspirational romance book club,* the only one featuring love stories where Christian faith is the primary ingredient in a marriage relationship.

Sign up today to receive your first set of four, never before published Christian romances. Send no money now; you will receive a bill with the first shipment. You may cancel at any time without obligation, and if you aren't completely satisfied with any selection, you may return the books for an immediate refund!

Imagine. . .four new romances every month—two historical, two contemporary—with men and women like you who long to meet the one God has chosen as the love of their lives. . .all for the low price of $9.97 postpaid.

To join, simply complete the coupon below and mail to the address provided. **Heartsong Presents** romances are rated G for another reason: They'll arrive *Godspeed!*